MONSTER STINK

ANNA BROOKE Illustrated by OWEN LINDSAY

2 Palmer Street, Frome,
Somerset BA11 1DS

First published in Great Britain in 2023
Chicken House
2 Palmer Street
Frome, Somerset BA11 1DS
United Kingdom
www.chickenhousebooks.com

Chicken House/Scholastic Ireland, 89E Lagan Road, Dublin Industrial Estate,
Glasnevin, Dublin D11 HP5F, Republic of Ireland

Designed and typeset by Steve Wells
Printed and bound in Great Britain by CPI Group (UK) Ltd, Croydon CR0 4YY

FSC
www.fsc.org
MIX
Paper | Supporting
responsible forestry
FSC® C171272

1 3 5 7 9 10 8 6 4 2

British Library Cataloguing in Publication data available.

PB ISBN 978-1-913696-59-7
eISBN 978-1-915026-90-3

For Pascal

Dear ⎯⎯⎯⎯⎯⎯⎯⎯⎯⎯⎯
(I don't know your name yet, so insert it here),

To read on you need to do three very important things.

FIRST: Promise you'll never ever show a grown-up this book. Grown-ups hate bogeys and smelly things (and this book is full of 'em), so they're bound to barf.

SECOND: You need to say 'hi' to our heroes, the Snozzlers, which is their stage name. Their real names are:

Frank Bear Horace Pickerty-Boop, recognizable by his ginger curls, and for having an index finger always ready for a root around his honker.

Tiffany, Frank's best friend, who never goes anywhere without her

Frank

-2-

Tiffany

acrobatic slugs, Sammy, Violet, Peach and Slim.

Frank's mum, who never misses a high note.

Frank's dad, who makes horror movies.

Bogey, the Star of the Show. He looks a right slimer of a monster, but don't be fooled. He's kind and friendly and very good with animals, like Binky and her performing bats, with whom he communicates using only his mind.

Bogey

THIRD: And this is VERY IMPORTANT, OK? You ABSOLUTELY MUST read the book warning below. Your life may depend on it, so PLEASE, PLEASE don't skip it.

BOOK WARNING

Please handle this book with care! Don't shake it, drop it or turn it upside down.

For inside is something very VERY dangerous – something known as the Stinkus-Dinkus-Inus-Nozzleus-Horriblis.

And it's whiffing and whirling about these pages like an invisible, nightmarish cloud.

Which pages?

I don't know, yet. Not this one. But definitely some others, so you must be VERY VERY careful.

One clumsy page turn and you could – POOOFF – find yourself breathing it in, which'd make you . . . Hmmm, I'd better not tell that bit. It might put you off reading. Let's just say that the

Stinkus-Dinkus-Inus-Nozzleus-Horriblis —
we'll just call it the Stink from now on —
has a very dangerous side effect.

And so, to read on, you will need:

✸ a nose peg

✸ something that smells nice — a chocolate
bar, a marshmallow, peanut butter, boiled
sprouts . . . (What? I love that smell!)

✸ a pack of tissues
and

✸ possibly a spare pair of underpants

Got it? Good.

Now, dearest stinkers — yes, that's you —
please turn to Chapter 1.

Oh, and listen . . .

There's music in Chapter 1 so you'll
probably be all right. Probably. Oh, I
don't know . . . just follow the notes . . .

FORGET THE REST, YOU'RE THE BEST

'**G**OOLIEMALOOLIE!** They're good,' whispered Frank, peering around the backstage curtain at the entertainers before them.

They were four musicians in leather trousers and sequinned science coats, a band called **LOBBO'S LAB RATS**. And what they were good at was singing showy, science-themed rock ballads, like 'I've Got My Ion You' and 'Love Knows No Cell-By Date', while balancing on moving motorcycles.

Frank's index finger crept up his nostril, as it always did when he felt nervous. 'Wow! How did they do that?' he whispered, as coloured smoke suddenly shot out of the Lab Rats' bikes' exhaust pipes and morphed into moving shapes like little dancers, before disappearing in a puff of glitter.

'Soaring slugs! That's gonna be a hard act to follow,' said Tiffany, Frank's best friend, as she stroked her performing circus slugs, Sammy, Violet, Peach and Slim, for reassurance.

'Goo,' agreed their monster friend Bogey, before slurping the glob-nugget Frank had just extracted from his nose. Eating bogeys soothed his pre-show jitters.

'Don't worry, our show's good *tooooooooo,*' sang Frank's mum operatically, clutching Dad's arm and trying to stay positive, but when Lobbo's deep, gravelly rock voice rose into an expertly controlled high-pitched falsetto, she gasped. 'Whoa! A top B!'

Tiffany recorded it on her phone. 'His group's definitely the best so far,' she whispered to Frank (who wasn't allowed a phone yet), 'so this way, we'll remember what we're up against if we happen to get through.'

'Oh, good idea,' said Dad, getting his phone out too. 'Why didn't I think of that?'

'Right,' Frank said, looking at his wristwatch, then up at the ceiling to check Binky and the other bats were in place. (They were.) 'Prepare yourselves, everybody. We're next.'

There was a lot riding on this performance.

For they were in none other than the famous Blob-Warble Theatre in the city of Warble-Blob, competing in the semi-finals of the most prestigious TV entertainment prize in the world: *FORGET THE REST, YOU'RE THE BEST*! If they made it through this round, they'd be in the FINAL. And if they won that, they'd get to perform all around the world this summer. And the idea of winning and travelling the globe with his best friends and family made Frank positively shiver with excitement. Maybe they'd even visit Paris, where his mum and dad had once lived – they'd told him so much about it.

After Lobbo had sounded his last high note, and his

band had done more daredevil motorcycle stunts, while singing 'We Love Heavy Metals' and juggling test tubes, **LOBBO'S LAB RATS** bowed to the TV cameras then left the stage to wild cheers and applause.

Frank wanted to say 'well done' as they passed (he thought it was the nice thing to do). But when he saw Lobbo up close, he suddenly lost his voice.

There was something about his glittery lab coat, blond quiff, platform shoes and gold hoop earring that gave Frank the willy-willy-woo-woos. (Or was it just his snarling face? Erm, yes, it was that.)

And Lobbo's show partners were scary too . . .

Lil Hunk, the muscly lead guitarist, did a nasty two-fingered prong movement, pointing at his own bloodshot eyes then aiming at Frank, as if to say, *I'm watching you.*

Daphne, the black-lipsticked second guitarist (and Lobbo's big sister) growled at Tiffany, before pointing at the words 'make 'em bleed', written in red sequins on her T-shirt.

Bendy Babs, the leggy red-headed lead dancer, rolled up

the sleeves of her silver lab coat to show off long, bright-pink nails like knives.

They were the most menacing-looking lot Frank had ever clapped eyes on.

'Soaring slugs! I've got the heebie-jeebies,' whispered Tiffany once they'd all gone past.

'MEEP,' agreed Sammy, Violet, Peach and Slim.

'Oh, I'm sure they're nice, really,' said Dad. 'They just want to win, so they're trying to unnerve us. It's classic competition behaviour.'

But Frank wasn't so sure. Bogey was shedding squidgepeas (squishy bogeys shaped like peas), which meant he was frightened, which meant he'd sensed nastiness.

But there was no time to say any more, 'cause suddenly a loud voice boomed across the stage.

'LADIES AND GENTLEMEN, BOYS AND GIRLS, PUT YOUR HANDS TOGETHER FOR THE LAST ACT OF THE SEMI-FINALS. THE FABULOUS, THE FANTASTICAL, THE MYSTERIOUS ... SNOZZLERS!'

Frank's heart beat faster at the sound of their name. He was the one who'd invented it and he was very proud.

The crowd roared.

The Snozzlers huddled together below the bats and chanted 'JUST PICK IT!' three times for luck (which sounded like 'MEEP MIP MIP' for the slugs), then ran out into their positions in front of the TV cameras: Bogey on a podium; Tiffany up front with the slugs; Mum at the back in front of a giant movie screen; Dad in the projection area and Frank backstage, making sure their show ran smoothly.

It was time to wow the judges.

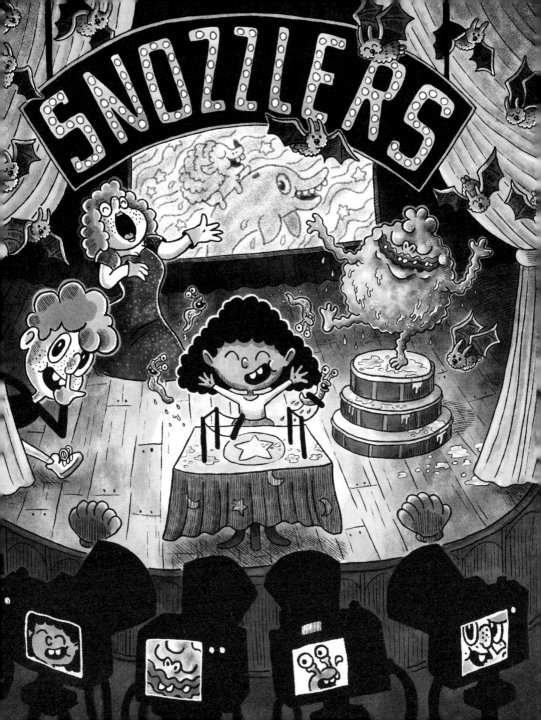

CHAPTER 2

A QUICK QUIZ

S tinkers, here's a quick quiz.

QUESTION NUMBER 1:

How do you think the Snozzlers' show went?

☐ **A. Like a half-eaten chicken drumstick in a brown sock.**

☐ **B. Like a raw, pink sausage on an underground train.**

☐ **C. REALLY REALLY WELL.**

If you answered C) REALLY REALLY WELL, then

you're REALLY REALLY wrong.

Whoops. No, sorry. You're not. You're TOTALLY spot on!

For when Mum opened their new spooky-themed show with her opera aria, 'Goo-goo-gooey' (in honour of Bogey), the crowds swooned.

When Dad showed his music video *Binky and his Amazing Technicolor Dreamwings* – a sensational Batway spectacular featuring Bogey and Binky, with special guest, Honkerty Village's weird hedgehog, performing 'Any Dream Will Goo' in dolphin (the hedgehog was an expert dolphin impersonator) – the audience gave a deafening cheer.

When the slugs, Sammy, Violet, Peach and Slim, swung on little trapezes in zombie suits, then catapulted through the air to land in a perfect tower on top of Tiffany's head (in a part of the act called *Attack of the Zombie Gastropods*), everyone went wild.

And when, for the finale, Bogey, from high up on his podium, choreographed a haunting aerial bat display led by Binky, which filled the entire theatre in ghostly, swirling light (the bats had little bulbs on their wings) that eventually formed the words '***FORGET THE REST, YOU'RE THE BEST***' in mid-air, the people proclaimed it the most magical thing they'd ever seen.

QUESTION NUMBER 2: *But was it enough to earn them a place in the final?*

Ooh, good question. And I don't know yet, 'cause the results aren't out. But they will be in about ten seconds, so if you go to the next chapter (watching out for **THE STINK**, remember) and start counting down, you're bound to find out.

CHAPTER 3

COUNTDOWN!

10.

The Snozzlers huddled together on the edge of the stage, alongside the other competitors,* their hearts beating a million-billion-zillion-gazillion miles an hour.

9.

Frank grabbed Tiffany's and Bogey's hands for comfort and took a deep breath. Binky fluttered down to sit on Bogey's shoulder.

---

* Stinkers, the other competitors were: the Gorgeous Goblins, a group of dancing magicians in – you got it – goblin suits; the Peanut Prancers, a strangely hypnotic act of hula-hoopers with giant peanut masks; the Sock Swindlers, a weird dance act dressed in costumes made of, erm . . . socks; and (of course) Lobbo's Lab Rats, who were a-pouting and a-posing like there was no tomorrow.

8.

Dicky Dingaling, **_FORGET THE REST, YOU'RE THE BEST_**'s famous, bald-headed judge, strode on to the stage carrying a big envelope.

7.

Judge Dingaling cleared his throat.

6.

Judge Dingaling opened the envelope.

5.

Judge Dingaling scratched his— Sorry, I can't say what he scratched. He'd forgotten he was in public. The audience hooted.

4.

Judge Dingaling carried on as if nothing had happened.

3.

Judge Dingaling drew out a card

from the envelope . . .

2.

. . . and shouted, 'Put your hands together for . . .'

'Please let it be us. Please, please, please,'

whispered Frank.

Bogey crossed his webbed fingers.

The slugs wrapped their tails around Tiffany's pinkie.

Binky and the bats fluttered nervously.

1.

'. . . our first winners, who are the Gorgeous Goblins!'

Frank hung his head!

No, he didn't! I'm having you on.

Judge Dingaling had screamed, **'THE SNOZZLERS'**!

And the second Frank heard their name, he felt his heart

leap out of his chest, grow wings and fly around the theatre

(don't worry, it went back in).

And the others were ECSTATIC too:

Tiffany and the slugs did dozens of high fives, until the slugs' eye tentacles got tangled.

Dad got out his phone and excitedly started filming the cheering crowds.

Mum sang, 'We got *throo-oo-ooo-uuuugh*!' in an impressive high A.

And Bogey and Binky's bats improvised a whole new bat choreography that left the audience speechless.

But there was still one group to announce, and in a flash, Judge Dingaling extracted a second card from the envelope and screamed, 'And facing the Snozzlers in the Grand Final are . . . **LOBBO'S LAB RATS**!'

The crowds went berserk. So did the Lab Rats, who howled and prowled and strutted their stuff like victorious peacocks in science coats.

Frank gasped. Tiffany had been right.

Well, he wasn't going to let *that* ruin their moment.

For they, the Snozzlers – the unlikely troupe with performing slugs, bats and the only bogey monster in the entire world – had GOT THROUGH! And as Frank held Tiffany's hand and looked into Bogey's gloopy yellow-green eyes, he felt sure that from now on, with his best friends and family by his side, anything was possible.

'**GOOLIEMALOOLIE!**' he shouted. 'This is the Best Day Eveeeeeer!'

CHAPTER 3½

WARNING!

Now, stinkers, you've probably noticed that the story so far has been all about **JOY** and **SUCCESS**.

Well, make the most of it, 'cause it's not going to last!

In fact, things are about to go downhill FAST. And when I say 'downhill FAST', I mean downhill like a **SPLAT-GLOB** (a bogey that falls out your nose, tumbles to the floor at high speed and lands with a big, fat SPLAT!).

For, you see, the Snozzlers were so caught up in their celebrating, that soon they'd forgotten all about the scary

Lab Rats, and failed to notice three VERY important things:

1) **LOBBO** observing Bogey from across the stage with a look of jealousy. Or was it curiosity? Or was it jealousy *and* curiosity mixed together? Hmmm, yes, 'twas that - a nasty little thing I call jealosity.
2) **LOBBO** sneakily following Bogey and the Snozzlers towards their dressing room.
3) **LOBBO** spying a faint Bogey footprint on the carpet and scraping some of it into one of his test tubes.

'Twas a massive shame, 'cause had the Snozzlers noticed any of this, they might have kept a better eye on Bogey

and our story would be different. And we'd all be tucked up in our beds (me with a midnight feast of fairy cakes and boiled sprouts, you with . . . nothing; you're too young to be up at midnight!), safe in the knowledge that nothing could stop the

Snozzlers on their way to the finals. But instead, here we are in this yucky yarn, worrying whether we'll get knocked out by **THE STINK** and spewing poetry to calm our nerves.

What lies ahead is nothing but woe
Don't say I didn't tell you so
Ouch. Oh no. I've stubbed my toe.

There. That's mine.

_____

_____

_____

_____

_____

And I've left you some space to write your own dazzling ditty.

Or perhaps you'd rather soothe your nerves with a snack.

A bag of Bally-Wally Balls should do it (everyone's heard about the comforting effects of green-coloured chocolate-coated bananas on a lolly stick).

Or I've recently discovered a delightful little fruit called a grape.

Whatever tickles your fancy.

You have been warned.

CHAPTER 4

A CHOICE

NOW, TO MOVE THIS STORY ALONG, STINKERS, YOU HAVE A CHOICE:

If you'd like to stay with the Snozzlers and accompany them on their boring drive back from Warble-Blob to Honkerty Village, then watch Tiffany go home and the others go straight to bed in Snozzle Castle, turn to page 244.

Or:

To find out more about Lobbo and his Lab Rats, shout...

POOP DECK!

... then turn the page.

Don't be shy. Forward time travel in this book only happens if you say silly things. Plus, poop deck doesn't have anything to do with number twos. It means the roof of a cabin at the back of a ship!

Honestly!

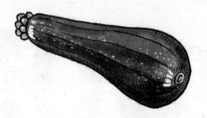

CHAPTER 5

PERFORMER'S POP

Well done (this was by far the best choice). And you've now travelled seven hours into the future, out of Warble-Blob, over the River Floop (pronounced Floop), across some fields, down an overgrown lane and into a deep dark wood, where it's the black of night.

Which wood?

A wood once called Fluffy Fairy Wood, but now called **PRIVATE PROPERTY – KEEP OUT OR DIE WOOD**.

And right in the middle of it is - shhhh! - a secret,

state-of-the-art concrete bunker with its own rooftop helipad, and – oh look, perfect timing – the **LAB RATS** themselves, driving up to it on their show bikes.

'We're gonna crush them Snozzlers next week, I can feel it in my copters,' croaked Lil Hunk, as the band stopped in some grass in front of a sheer wall. He got off his motorbike and used his bulging, helicopter-tattooed arms to twist a football-sized rock in the grass.

HISSSSSSS

The wall moved apart and the Lab Rats drove into their secret tunnel.

'Yeah, crush 'em like flies,' rasped Bendy Babs, snapping her knife-like nails together with a clickety-clack. 'We were well good!'

'Oy, Rubber-Legs, I'll crush you like flies if you don't park in your spot,' Daphne grunted as she pushed her own bike towards a space marked 'Daphne' at the end of the tunnel. She was fed up of Bendy leaving her bike around.

Bendy huffed. She hated tidying. 'OK, but if I break a nail, you're dead.'

'Now, now, Lab Rats. No arguing,' cried Lobbo, leaping off his very shiny silver bike. 'Not when we have so much work ahead of us.'

He strutted over to the bunker's voice-activated front door and sang an excellent top B into a little box.

The door unlocked with a **beep** and Lobbo swept through. 'Come on, Rats,' he ordered. He'd got a nasty plan brewing . . .

The Lab Rats finished parking and followed Lobbo down the long, stark, concrete corridor past:

* a door marked *Lobbo's Science Station*
* a soundproofed *Tune Room*
* ultramodern dressing rooms
* computerized toilets with self-heating seats
* a high-tech greenhouse filled with five-metre-long courgettes (Lobbo's favourite vegetable)
* a huge sealed room marked *Danger! Enter at Your Own Risk*
* a button on the wall marked *Bunker Destruction – For Emergency Only* (there was one in each room)

(Bear with me. We're almost there – the bunker was massive.)

. . . into the state-of-the-art kitchen, where four robotic hands immediately descended from the ceiling to serve them a glass of **Performer's Pop**© – a well-impressive fizzy drink Lobbo had invented. It took on different flavours according to your mood:

* **Sly – courgette and raspberry**
* **Worried – courgette and banana**
* **Jealous – courgette and cherry**
* **Excited – courgette and strawberry**

(It contained lots of courgette, of course, plus honey and a secret ingredient I'll share with you if you give me a packet of cheese and onion crisps right now. *What? You haven't got any? Well, sorry. Maybe next time.*)

'Don't worry, Lab Rats, we *are* going to crush them,' said Lobbo with a flick of his quiff. 'Mmm, courgette and raspberry!' He took another sip. 'Just not in the way you think. You see . . .' He paused for dramatic effect. **'AS THINGS STAND, THE SNOZZLERS ARE GOING TO**

WIN!'

'Whaaaat?' cried Lil Hunk, Daphne and Bendy in perfect harmony, suddenly tasting courgette and banana.

'Oh, don't get me wrong. We are brilliant,' said Lobbo, looking up at the glass cabinets on the wall where their performance trophies were displayed next to his science invention certificates. 'The problem's not us. It's that sticky little man.'

'But all he did was stupid tricks with bats,' said Lil Hunk.

'Yeah,' said Bendy, giving Lil Hunk a big sloppy kiss on the cheek. (I forgot to say, Bendy was Lil Hunk's girlfriend. I know - yuck!)

'Not *stupid* tricks!' Lobbo felt a ball of jealousy swell in his chest (and a courgette and cherry flavour in his mouth). 'Very *impressive* tricks. Never underestimate your enemy. We may be brilliant performers and I am most definitely a genius. But even I don't know how to choreograph a hundred *Pipistrellus pipistrellus*.'

'Pipi what?' asked Lil Hunk.

'The bats!' snapped Lobbo with an eye roll. Sometimes

being the most intelligent person in the group was a chore. 'It's the scientific name for their bats!'

'But the judges loved us,' said Bendy. 'We got through, didn't we?'

'Yes. But the judges loved *them* too and chose them first. And because of that bat stuff – if I do the maths –' Lobbo's genius eyes rolled up towards his blond quiff as he murmured some figures – 'the Snozzlers have a **99.99999999999997** per cent chance of winning.'

'Wha—?' sang Lil Hunk, Bendy and Daphne all at once.

'Don't panic!' Lobbo interrupted with a wicksmirk (the official name for a 'wicked smirk'). He drew out a test tube of Bogey's footprint scrapings. 'A quick analysis of the sticky man's prints has given me an idea. And so we're going to win that competition by—'

'Doing a brilliant TV report?' Bendy blurted. A crew were meeting them in a nearby theatre later that day to do a piece on them (before heading to the Snozzlers the next morning). It would be broadcast on TV on the night of the live final and Bendy couldn't wait to show off her new moves.

Daphne elbowed her. 'Don't interrupt!'

Bendy flashed her sharp pink fingernails.

'No, better than that,' Lobbo continued, ignoring the bickering. 'We're going to win that competition by . . .'

He paused, savouring the taste of courgette and strawberry . . .

'CAUSING CHAOS!'

CHAPTER 6

SCHLOP!

Meanwhile – or actually, twelve hours later ('cause the Snozzlers had sleep to catch up on after that boring drive I bet you insisted on reading more about earlier, and lay in 'til mid-afternoon) – Frank, Tiffany, Bogey, Mum, Dad and the slugs were sitting in Snozzle Castle's cosy, wood-panelled kitchen.

What were they doing there?

Having a whale of a time around the dining table writing songs and creating mood boards for the final leg of the competition in two days' time.

ERM. NOT QUITE.

They were staring at blank whiteboards on the kitchen wall and having a proper old panic.

Why?

'Cause . . .

SCHLOP!

Did you hear that?

SCHLOP!

There it is again.

After all that winning and rejoicing and feeling as though nothing could stop them, they'd realized that to win the final, they were going to have to do it all again in forty-eight hours – except, they had been told by Judge Dingaling, with an even **bigger** and **better show**. And all that extra stress was sucking their good ideas straight out of their brains like a vacuum – **SCHLOP! SCHLOP! SCHLOP!**

'**GOOLIEMALOOLIE!**' – **SCHLOP!** – 'I can't think of anything good!' declared Frank, picking his nose for comfort and finally scratching off a clingenglob (an awkward booger that just won't budge). It had been there since before the semi-final. *At least that's one good thing,* he thought.

Dad went to share his thoughts, but – **SCHLOP!** – they vanished, so he tinkered with a vintage camera lens he'd just bought.

Mum went to sing a new song idea, but – **SCHLOP!** – it disappeared, so she stared into the oven at the chocolate and broccoli muffins she was determined not to burn.

Tiffany went to explain a new slug move, but – **SCHLOP!** – she couldn't remember what it was, so Sammy, Violet, Peach and Slim did their usual zombie poses.

And Bogey went to say **'GOO!'** (which meant, 'I know what we should do, we should . . .'), but – **SCHLOP!** – his idea evaporated too, so he gobbled the clingenglob Frank had mined and told Binky and the bats to have a rest in the rafters.

'Well, let's not worry just yet,' said Dad, trying to sound positive and passing Bogey one of his own little nose nuggets. 'Ideas often come when you least expect it, not when you try to force them.'

'Yes, but that TV crew's coming in the morning, to film us for that piece for the final, remember?' said Tiffany.

'That only leaves us today and part of tomorrow.'

'Oh, this is impossible,' said Frank, getting up from his chair to jump up and down (jumping helped him think). 'I bet Lobbo's lot aren't having any trouble.'

They weren't, stinkers, but more about that later.

'Nothing's impossible, *sweetheaaaaaaaaart*,' sang Mum, reaching into the oven to extract the only-slightly-burnt muffins and dropping them on the floor.

Any other day, Frank would have chortled like a chimp. Today, he just helped her pick them up in silence. He knew she was right. Bogey's very existence was proof that anything was possible. But this time things felt different. Since they'd entered ***FORGET THE REST, YOU'RE THE BEST***, Frank's passion for the Snozzlers' shows had gone from **THIS BIG** to

THIS BIG.

And since the semi-finals last night, the only thing he could think of was **WINNING** the **FINAL** and going around the world on the show tour with Bogey, Tiffany and his family by his side. They didn't know which cities the winners would play in yet, but Frank hoped Paris would be on the list. Mum and Dad had told him so many stories about it, and he'd always wondered what it was like. And yet here they were without a single-wingle, slopping-whopping, picking-wicking, sneezing-wheezing, bogey-wogey of an idea!

'I need some fresh air,' Frank sighed. Maybe a change of scenery would help the **SCHLOPS** to **STOP**. 'Tiffany, Bogey? Coming?'

DANGER ALERT!
DANGER ALERT!

GOODNESS ME, STINKERS!

I wasn't expecting this to happen so early in the story. **SORRY!** But something tells me you're about to

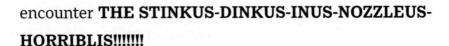

encounter **THE STINKUS-DINKUS-INUS-NOZZLEUS-HORRIBLIS!!!!!!!**

THE STINK.

What! So soon?

Yes. **URGH!** I know.

I said be ready for it, but I didn't think that'd mean **NOW**.

Oh well. There's no turning back. You'd better grab everything on the checklist on page 5.

FAST!!!!!

This is it. Things only get worse from here on. **OK? GOOD LUCK!**

CHAPTER 7

SIGN THIS TOMATO!

Walk, walk, walk.

Think. Think. Think.

Frank, Tiffany (slugs in jar) and Bogey walked walked walked and thunk thunk thunk (sorry, I mean 'thinked'. No, I mean 'thought'!) all around Snozzle Castle's gardens. But even after a hop around the moat (where the giant eel blew a few bubbles to say hello), a skip around the orchard and a jump past the greenhouse, the schlops were still a-schlopping and no one was any closer to having a good idea.

'We could head into the village,' suggested Tiffany.

'Goo,' said Bogey, which meant, 'Let's go.'

So off they went.

But unbeknown to the friends, the entire village had watched the Snozzlers perform on TV, so when they arrived at Honkerty-Honk-Honk (the silly name for the village's high street), the villagers all came flooding out of the shops and houses to congratulate them.

'Ooh, you did so well last night,' cried Mrs Wirrel, holding her five giant poodles on a short lead as she shook Frank's and Tiffany's hands. Then she turned to Bogey with a coy look. 'And you? Well, I just love you— Eh-hem, I mean... I love what you do with those bats!'

'Not as much as me,' said Walter Wills the grocer, pushing past Mrs Wirrel. 'Will you sign this tomato for me?' He handed Bogey a pen marked 'Number One Fan'.

Bogey obliged.

'And are you going to star in another one of Mr Pickerty-Boop's cool swamp monster films?' Bo Jacobs the street performer asked Bogey excitedly, as Squishy his dancing

hamster vied for Bogey's attention by doing an extra-difficult foxtrot on the pavement.

'And will you say "goo-goo-gooey" for me?' swooned Mrs Sniff, the Pickerty-Boops' elderly neighbour.

'**Goo-goo-gooey,**' said Bogey, pretending to jump out at her.

Mrs Sniff giggled so hard she accidentally spat out her false teeth.

There was no denying it. Bogey was the village star.

And Frank couldn't help but marvel at it. Not months earlier he'd been worried about how even his parents would react to his snotty friend. Bogey had been terrified about being seen in public. Now, here they all were, out in the open as celebrated performers, surrounded by people who loved them. It was as if Bogey's natural kindness had charmed the whole village.

'Say **"CHEESE!"**,' said Bo Jacobs, whipping out his camera.

'**GHEEEEEEESE!**' said Bogey, with Squishy breakdancing on his head.

Frank couldn't have felt prouder, and he could tell Bogey was loving the attention. But, right now, they had work to do.

'Sorry, guys. We've got to go,' he said, pushing through the crowds. 'To the fields,' he whispered to Tiffany and Bogey.

They really needed somewhere calm to think.

But alas, it wasn't to be.

As they edged around the perimeter of Gary Plonk's sweetcorn fields, the farmer shouting **'CONGRATULATIONS'** from his tractor as he started watering his crops, the schlops were still a-schlopping, and then, suddenly –

QUICK, STINKERS, EMERGENCY EQUIPMENT TIME!

PUT YOUR NOSE PEG ON NOOOOOOW!

– the most horrendous stink wafted into their nostrils. Frank thought he'd faint.

It was like crusty socks, stuffed with garlic, mixed with mouldy meat and bad breath and the poop of Fergus the smelly field mouse (who's one proper whiffer, I tell you). Though Frank had never met Fergus, so he just thought it was crusty socks, stuffed with garlic, mixed with mouldy meat and bad breath and the noxious whiff of . . .

'*Urgh . . . rotten eggs.* Tiffany, was that you?'

'NO IT WAS NOT!' she spluttered. 'Blurgh!' She covered her nose and mouth with her T-shirt. 'Bogey, was it you?'

'GAHHH!' exclaimed Bogey (which meant, 'NOOOOOO!'), rolling his yellow-green eyes.

The friends looked around to see if Plonk had noticed it too, but it didn't look like it; he was still busy spraying water.

And yet the smell was getting worse. Even the slugs looked woozy.

'**QUICK!**' cried Frank. '**RUN AWAY!**'

CHAPTER 8

THE STINK

But **THE STINK** was everywhere. By the time the friends got back to Snozzle Castle, the air was thick with it and everyone had to wear pegs on their noses and help close the castle's windows.

And all across Honkerty Village, **THE STINK** was making the villagers close other things too.

Mrs Sniff closed her mouth and her nose and set a new world record for little-old-lady breath-holding (1.57 seconds).

Bo Jacobs stuffed Squishy into his pocket, rushed

home, then closed himself (and the Squish-gal) inside the bathroom, packing towels under the door to stop **THE STINK** from getting in.

Mrs Wirrel, who was busy arguing with Walter Wills about who loved Bogey the most, went, 'URGH! What's tha—?', then closed the conversation mid-sentence and raced her poodles home, leaving Water Wills to quickly close his shop.

As for Farmer Plonk, **THE STINK** had hit him almost as soon as Frank, Tiffany and Bogey had run home, and he was now closed in his barn, sitting on a bag of Boblo's Grow Pellets, with no idea how to get home.

'Close all your doors and anything else that needs closing,' came a policeman's voice over a megaphone. It wasn't really a policeman. It was Honkerty's weird hedgehog. He'd been learning to impersonate policemen and megaphones (and even ambulance drivers), and was getting rather good at it. But nobody knew that. And it was good advice. So within half an hour, anyone who hadn't yet closed what they needed to close had finally closed it, and Honkerty Village looked like a ghost town.

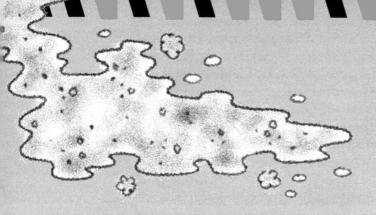

WARNING!

Are you scared yet, stinkers? You should be. For don't be fooled: **THE STINK** wasn't just disgusting, it was about to trigger a set of events both terrifying and dangerous, and only the following poem – which I wrote to calm my nerves – can describe it:

'Twas a dangerous stink, dear friend!
'Twas a disgusting stink, dear stranger!
'Twas a dangerous, disgusting stink all right.
Now everyone's in grave danger!
BLUUURGH, BLU-BLURGH, BLU-BLURGH
BLU-BLUUURGH, BLU-BLURGH, BLU-BLURGH
'Twas a dangerous, disgusting stink all right.
Now everyone's in— Oh, yes please, I'd like chips with my boiled sprouts. Lovely. Thank you.

Sorry, that last line's what I said on the phone to my favourite takeaway, Sprouty-Sprouty, as I was finishing the poem.

But the poem speaks the truth. For everyone *was* in grave danger. And you are too!

CHAPTER 9

OFF HIS BOGEYS!

That night, the mysterious Stink seemed to hover over Honkerty Village like a toxic cloud. Even with all the doors and windows closed, you could still smell it. And even with a peg on your nose, you could taste it.

Worse, the stench seemed stronger around Snozzle Castle, and the villagers had started calling to tell the Pickerty-Boops that there was a problem with the castle's sewers.

'I think you should get them checked,' said Mrs Wirrel.

'I'm a huge Snozzlers fan, but it's upsetting my poodles.'

'Please do call a plumber. No one'll come to my shop tomorrow if this continues,' said Walter Wills the grocer, adding, 'Oh and say hi to Bogey for me.'

'I beg you, do something! Clawdia my Siamese cat won't eat her din-dins,' pleaded old Mrs Sniff, before crying, **'GOO-GOO-GOOEY!'**

'It's bound to pass,' said Frank, trying to stay positive as Dad put down the phone and the Snozzlers all sat around the kitchen table again for dinner and a think. They really needed to come up with ideas for the final. But between **THE STINK** and the calls, it was proving impossible.

Even more worryingly, Bogey was suddenly off his bogeys. When Frank gave him his plate, he pushed it away. And when he asked him what was wrong, he just growled angrily and gritted his peggy teeth, which hurt Frank's feelings.

Then when Tiffany asked him the same, he blew a raspberry and flicked a chumpclump at her (a small cluster of bogeys).

'What's going on?' she whispered to Frank.

'Dunno,' he replied. 'I've never seen him like this before.'

'I'd better leave the slugs with you tonight,' Tiffany said with a worried air. 'The TV crew's coming tomorrow morning, and the slugs' goo always makes Bogey feel better.'

'Good idea,' said Frank.

What on earth was wrong with Bogey? Was it something Frank'd done? It made him feel as unsettled as a hoverglob (you know, those bogeys that hover on the edge of your nostril – neither out nor in, about to fall, any second).

A tickle in his nose was telling him something was seriously wrong.

And when it came to Bogey, Frank's tickle was always right . . .

CHAPTER 9 ⅔

SPOILER ALERT!

U p in his new bedroom at the top of the dolled-up bell tower (decorated with nose-patterned wallpaper to make him feel at home), Bogey stomped and whomped and stamped his snotty feet. He **Grrred** and **Gaaaed** and **Goooed** and **Giiied**, and felt so strangely cross that when Frank went up to bring him the slugs, he cried **'GOO AGAAA!'** ('GO AWAY!') so hard that Frank left the slugs in a bucket by Bogey's bed and scarpered.

A little later, when the family was fast asleep, Bogey stared out of the window all hot and bothered, and – most unlike his normal self – frightened the owls with a **grrrrr!**

And then the full moon came out. So he **grrred** at that too.

And the more he **grrred** at it, the more it seemed to say *'Take off your nose peg, Bogey. Breathe in* **THE STINK**.'

So he did.

And then his eyes rolled back and his body shook and his nose tickled and

he got even angrier and:

'A-CHOOOOO!' A big sneeze splatted on his mirror.

Go on, Bogey, the moon seemed to say. *Break some stuff.*

So, he did. He smashed the mirror and a wooden chair and a vase of Green Balls, his favourite flowers (lime-green and round, like fluffy bogeys).

None of this was the moon, of course. Moons can't talk or make you sneeze. I hope you know that. No –

****SPOILER ALERT, SPOILER ALERT****

– it was **THE STINK!**

Though I bet you've already guessed that, haven't you, you clever stinkers?

But Bogey neither knew nor cared. All he wanted to do was growl and break stuff and SNOT all over his nice room.

So he did.

CHAPTER 10

PHASE TWOOOOOOOOOOOO!

Now, can you hear that, stinkers?

The distant sound of nasty snickering?

Hmmm. I think it's coming from outside. Let's take a look, shall we?

Ah yes.

Just as I thought.

While Bogey was busy destroying his room and the rest of Snozzle Castle was fast asleep, a burly tattooed man, two women (one with long pointy nails, the other with black lipstick) and a bloke with a blond quiff and a hoop earring were sitting in the shadows next to Farmer

Plonk's field, all wearing high-tech gasmasks.

And what they were doing was laughing their heads off as they zoomed in on Snozzle Castle with their power binoculars and saw Bogey's dark, angry silhouette sneezing snot against the golden light of his room in the bell tower.

'I can't believe you pulled it off,' said Lil Hunk between snorts.

''Course he did,' said Daphne, slapping her brother hard on his back. 'He always does.'

'That I do,' said Lobbo, wicksmirking while rubbing his back (Daphne didn't know her own strength). 'Phase one of the **STINKUS-DINKUS-INUS-NOZZLEUS-HORRIBLIS** is officially complete. I used the snotster's foot scrapings to make the formula, so if my calculations are correct, he'll soon be so sneezy and nasty, he'll ruin the Snozzlers' TV report in the morning!' He did a little swirl. 'Correction: he'll be so sneezy and DANGEROUS, he'll ruin the Snozzlers' report in the morning *and* won't be in the final. Then we'll be ready.'

The **LAB RATS** snickered even more nastily.

'HA!' Lobbo said. 'Winning this competition's going to be easius-peasius-lemonius-squeazius.'

'Will it make everyone else sneeze and go grumpy too?' asked Lil Hunk with a hopeful snort.

'Who knows?' Lobbo wicksmirked, again. 'It's bound to affect humans, I just don't know how yet 'cause I tailor-made it for the monster. But who cares! Just keep your masks on so *you* don't breathe it in. Right, my faithful ratties, it's checklist time. Special equipment?'

'Check!' Bendy did the splits, tapping a big box with her toes.

'Show-off,' muttered Daphne.

'Costumes ready?'

'Check!' Daphne lifted a huge bulging bag.

'Long ropes?'

'Check!' cried Lil Hunk, swinging a coil of cord around his thick arm, then throwing it at Bendy, who leapt up and caught it in mid-air with her leg, which was now by her ear.

Daphne rolled her eyes.

'Oh goodie!' Lobbo grinned, before crooning into his

gasmask mic in his most fabulous, controlled rock voice:

'Lab Rats, I'm so clever.
So clever, through and through.
Lab Rats, fame is coming!
Get ready for phase twooooooooooooo!'

FIRE AWAY!

I know what you're about to say:

'Well blow me over with a brown sock! Lobbo's the one behind **THE STINK**? We thought he might be, but now we KNOW he is!'

To which I say: 'OH YES.'

And if you're anything like me, you've got a question or two about it too, so go on. Fire away:

Great! OK. So, no one knows what the Stink'll do to humans yet, but how does it work on Bogey?

Good question. Press this snot ball and I'll show you what I know:

There you go. It's a special snot ball that lets you see inside people's bodies, like a microscope ('cause you won't be able to see what's going on with just the naked eye).

Look: these are normal cells (you know, the little tiny building blocks that make up everyone's bodies; you and Bogey probably have more than 37 trillion of 'em, which is A LOT).

Inside Bogey they're called **goodies**, and as you can see, they're perfectly round and smooth.

Goodies

But look what the Stink's doing to them.

It's morphing 'em into dark emerald cells called **wobblers**, with wobbly edges and teeny-weeny sparks of electricity crackling out of them, like microscopic lightning, which is bad news, 'cause once the wobblers multiply (which they've ALREADY started doing) they're going to start changing him in every way. I mean, you've already seen

Wobblers ⟶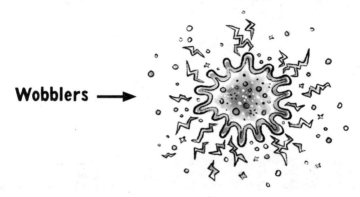

him grumpy and sneezy and growling, and who knows what else will happen.

Gosh, that's awful. Why would Lobbo do this?

Ah. Another good question.

And to answer it, I'm going to have to tell you a story. It's a little story within this story, something known in the storytelling business as a STO-story-RY.

It's called: '**How and why a genius scientist became a dangerous, all-singing, all-dancing crook with his own troupe of shady characters, entered *FORGET THE REST, YOU'RE THE BEST!* and wants to win it at ANY cost...**'

CHAPTER 12

ONCE UPON A TIME...

...there lived a scientist called Brian Bloob. He was an absolute brain-bags who wanted nothing more than to be rich and famous. And so, with the help of his lab assistant (his big sis Daphne), he invented all sorts of cool stuff, like...

* **A machine that turns old cheese into stretchy underpants.**
* **A boot with its own air-heating system to keep your feet warm.**
* **An ultra-speedy sausage maker with an output of**

15,000 sizzlers a minute.

And thanks to his inventions, Brian Bloob was soon wack 'em rack 'em rolling in it.

So that was the rich part sorted.

But the fame part was MUCH more difficult.

Ever heard of Brian Bloob before reading this page?

Exactly!

And it was driving him wild!

'It's driving me wild!' he cried one day as a ball of bitterness swelled in his chest.

'Cause it was.

And then he had a proper tantrum on the floor.

But once the tantrum had stopped (and Daphne had hairsprayed his silky blond quiff back into place), a terrible idea whooshed into his mind.

WHOOOSH!!!

Did you get it?

No?

WHOOOSH!

There it goes again.

Still no?

OK, I'll tell you.

If Brian Bloob couldn't get famous by inventing helpful things, he'd do it by inventing . . .

SOMETHING TERRIBLE!

HIPPOPOTAMOUSE

C an you guess what it was?

❇ **A toaster that shouts rude words when the bread's ready?**

❇ **A hippopotamouse, which is a cross between a hippo and a mouse and about the size of a small dog?**

❇ **A remote-controlled clothes-loosening device that leaves everybody standing with their underpants round their ankles?**

Nah, of course it was **THE STINK** (though Bloob did

actually make all of the above – even the hippopotamouse, who lives . . . erm, nobody knows where any more).

And Bloob's cutting-edge cell-changing technology was so dangerous, illegal AND whiffy, that the Science Board – which makes sure all science experiments respect the law – caught wind of it (quite literally) and told him to stop.

'**STOP!**' they ordered, in a very official letter delivered by a policeman called Phil.

But Bloob wasn't going to let PC Phil or a stuffy institution like the Science Board shut him down. Not when the sweet jingle-jangle of fame was ringing in his ears.

So, on he went with his Stink invention.

But the only fame Bloob got was a tiny article in a little-known newspaper called the *Trifle Times* (which collapsed straight after), about an unimportant scientist who got sent to Bing Bang High-Security Prison for three years by PC Phil for an illegal, proper-whiffy science experiment.

CHAPTER 14

CHOPPER CHOPPER CHOPPER

Now, prison ain't fun. Remember that!

'What you in for?' came a gruff voice on Bloob's first day, as the cell door clanged behind him.

Bloob spun round trembling to see a massive tattooed man sitting on the top bunk.

'I'm Lil Hunk. I'm in for armed robbery and stealing helicopters!' said the man proudly with a nasty gurgle in his throat. 'I love copters…' He laughed like a weird donkey. 'And this is my girlfriend, Babs.' He leapt off the bunk and handed Bloob a photo of a red-headed woman with long, knife-like nails, doing the splits. 'Ain't she pretty? I call her Bendy, 'cause she has proper stretchy legs.'

Bloob wanted to scream **'GET ME OUT OF HERE!'** and have a tantrum on the floor, but Daphne wasn't there for his hair, so he pretended he was tough instead.

'Cheer up,' said Lil Hunk. 'I've only been in three fights since yesterday, so I've been given good behaviour rights with this.' He reached under the bottom bunk, pulled out a battered guitar and sang a rock number he'd written for Bendy.

'I'll fly my copter to yo-oo-oou,
Like you want me to-oo-oo.
Whirl, whirl, whirl,
My rotor's in a swirl,
'Cause I-I-I love you girl.'

'Oh, woe is me!' said Bloob, accidentally out loud.

But when Lil Hunk got to the chorus – *'chopper, chopper, chopper'* – something **UTTERLY MAJORLY MASSIVELY UNEXPECTED** happened inside Bloob's head.

- 72 -

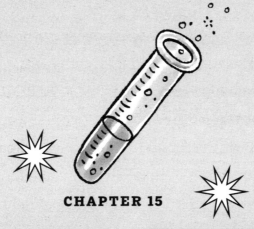

CHAPTER 15

0.000001 SECONDS

FRAZZLE CRACK!

Did you hear it?

'Twas the sound of electricity sizzling through Brian Bloob's brain as the weirdly catchy refrain made parts of his mind feel alive in ways not even the whiffy invention he'd gone to prison for had made him feel. And in seconds, despite himself and his fear, he found himself singing along.

'Chopper, chopper - ahhhhhhhhhhhh
Chopper, chopper, ooh-ahhhhhhhhhhhh.'

And soon he'd forgotten himself.

So much that when Lil Hunk stopped, he carried on.

And shook his hips.

And tweaked his quiff.

And improvised a flurry of notes that ended in a spectacular top B that lasted 59.7 seconds.

'Blimey, where'd you learn to sing like that?' said Lil Hunk, open-jawed.

'Yeah!' came a chorus of voices from five prison guards peering in through the bars. The sound of applause poured out of the surrounding cells (they housed five murderers, ten bank robbers and two dog-snatchers).

'I-I-I . . .' For the first time in his life, Brian Bloob didn't know what to say. He'd never even tried singing before. His entire life had only ever been about science, science, science. Could it be that he was good at music too?

He paused for 0.000001 seconds to think about it.

Of course he was good at it. He was a genius. Notes were to music what molecules were to science* - the building blocks of everything. And he could pretty much do what he wanted with molecules! That's how he made **THE STINK**! If his calculations were correct, he'd have this music lark mastered in five minutes and his voice properly trained in ten.

And do you know what? He did.

And for the rest of his prison sentence, he wrote songs and sang with Lil Hunk every day. And changed his name to something much showier:

Brian Elvis di Lobbo, or for short – just Lobbo.

And then one day, it was time to leave prison and Lobbo could feel that familiar craving for FAME tap-dancing on his bum again. (Don't ask me why it tap-danced there, stinkers, it just did.)

'I know how to make us famous,' Lobbo shouted back to Lil Hunk as the prison officers escorted him towards the exit. 'Music is my master now. My sister Daphne's built a

---

* Know what molecules are? Clue. They're smaller than cells. They're the teeny-tiny-weeny ingredients that make up almost everything on Earth: the air we breathe, your cat, your dog, your teacher, your pants, your teacher's pants, your bogeys, the moon, this book . . . even the Stink (and the nose peg I hope you're still wearing).

brilliant bunker for us. See you on the *outsiiiiiiiide!*'

It was a proper mouthful shouting all that back, but he'd just about managed it and Lil Hunk had caught all the main bits.

And so, as the prison gate swung closed behind him, out went Lobbo - the artist formerly known as Brian Bloob - with a flick of his quiff, dead set on getting **MEGA-ULTRA-BIGTIME FAMOUS.**

And this time, he thought, *I'll let nothing - and I mean **NOTHING** - stand in my way.*

RHINOTILLEXOMANIA

So there you have it, stinkers.

That's why Lobbo's being a rotter and has targeted Bogey and the Snozzlers with his **STINKUS-DINKUS-INUS-NOZZLEUS-HORRIBLIS**.

Though how he's got his Stink into the air around Honkerty Village is quite beyond me.

Any ideas? Drop me an email: author@i-never-pick-my-nose-ever-honestly.com.

Though I'm sure we'll find out later. Probably ... Maybe ... Oh, I don't know.

But where was I?

Oh yes. We were about to travel forwards in time again – to see how all this is affecting Frank, Tiffany and Bogey – with a proper long word this time.

Shout

RHINOTILLEXOMANIA.

(Sorry, but I don't choose them. Binky the bat chose this one, so blame her.)

Rhinotillexomania is the proper scientific word for what (as my email address suggests) I never ever do, but for what you do at least 173 times a day: pick your hooter!

Go on, shout it.

And break it down if it's a mouthful. Not your bogeys! I hope you don't eat those. Only Bogey's allowed to do that. I meant the word:

RHINO-TILL-EXO-MANIA

Ah, brilliant. And now you've flown forward to the morning after **THE STINK**, which is also the day before the final.

Now, sniff the air.

It's filled with the sweet aroma of freshly cut grass, cherry tomatoes and vanilla marshmallows.

No, sorry. It's not.

The air's still as whiffy as crusty socks, stuffed with garlic, mixed with mouldy meat and bad breath and the poop of Fergus the smelly field mouse.

CHAPTER 16

WHOPPING GREENIES

'**G**ooliema—!'

'Soaring slu—!'

When Frank and Tiffany went up to the bell tower to check on Bogey the morning after **THE STINK** had begun, they couldn't get their words out - not because **THE STINK** was still in the air (though, as you know, it was). But because never before had they seen such a gloop fest (which, for two children who'd once wiped snot all over Honkerty Village, was saying something).

Every centimetre of Bogey's room - floor, walls and

ceiling – was smothered in giant splats of whopping greenies.

But worse of all, amid the broken, dripping furniture, growling at something, was Bogey, with a dangerous glint in his yellow-green eyes.

WORSER STILL. He was growling at the SLUGS!

Tiffany immediately scooped them out of the bucket. They were trembling like jelly. She dropped them gently into their jar, where they hid under a lettuce leaf. 'It's OK fellas,' she cooed, before turning to Frank with a look of alarm.

'Are they all right?' Frank asked.

'I think so.'

'Y-you feeling OK, Bogey?' Frank said. For the first time in his life, his usual nose tickle felt as hot as fire, which was making him feely shaky too. 'What happened? It looks like you've been breaking stuff and sling-snotting bits of yourself everywhere. And why did you frighten the slugs?'

Bogey didn't answer. Instead, he leapt towards the friends shouting, **'GRRRRRR!'**

'WHOA!' Frank and Tiffany jumped back, grabbing Bogey's bed to avoid slipping in the goop.

'OK, Bogey. Calm down,' Frank said, his stomach clenching as that 'unsettled hoverglob' feeling came back.

Why was Bogey being so mean? What on earth was going on?

'The TV people'll be here in an hour,' he went on, picking his nose nervously and offering Bogey a whopper of a glob-nugget. 'Maybe this'll help put you right.' A good snack usually made him smile.

But Bogey just batted Frank's hand away, before letting out a massive sneeze – **A-A-GHOOOOOOO!** – which whizzed through the air and splatted on an upturned armchair.

'Maybe this is what happens when he's got a cold?' Tiffany whispered. 'He gets grumpy, goes off his food – he didn't eat dinner last night either, did he? – and produces extra snot, which he sneezes everywhere?'

'Could be,' said Frank, trying not to feel upset. But a little voice in his head was telling him it wasn't that at all.

It wasn't his own voice. It was a dust mite in his left ear. But Frank didn't know that and it'd said exactly the same thing he was thinking (before leaping out, 'wheeeeee!' and landing in the floor goo, 'nooooooo!' SQUELCH!), so Frank said: 'Or – I've started to wonder if it isn't this weird Stink.'

'Go on,' said Tiffany.

'Well, Bogey started to get grumpy just after we'd smelt it by Farmer Plonk's field. And it's still strong now. Though I can't think why it would affect Bogey like this and not us.'

(Though it is affecting them too, isn't it, stinkers? They're not sneezy or grumpy, but . . . oh, I don't know. You'll just have to wait and see.)

'But everyone thinks it's Snozzle Castle's sewers,' Tiffany reminded him. Her hands were trembling. Frank had never seen her so spooked.

'Well, I s'pose it could be. But what if they're wrong? We had a blocked loo in the castle last week, remember, and nothing like this happened.'

'GRRRRRRRR!'

The two friends spun around to find Bogey suddenly perched on his bed, fixing them with angry eyes. And – **'GOOLIEMALOOLIE!'** – HE'D GROWN!

'How did—?' yelped Frank in a whisper (something I call a whisp-yelp). He was lost for words. Everything about Bogey's body was suddenly thicker and gloopier and taller, by about a foot. 'I don't think a cold or a sewer smell would

make that happen.'

'S-soaring s-slugs! Nor do I!' Tiffany whisp-yelped back, clutching the slug jar close to her chest and looking panicky. 'Do you think we should tell your mum and dad?'

'Yes . . . I mean no . . . Well, not yet. They've got enough on their plates worrying about what we're going to perform for the final tomorrow.' He thought back to how stressed the **SCHLOPS** had made them feel. 'Let's keep this secret for now and see if we can't find out more about **THE STINK** first . . . at Plonk's field. It's where we first smelt it. If we find something there, we might be able to get Bogey back to normal before the TV crew arrives and before Mum and Dad even know there's been a problem.'

It's a long shot, he thought, *but we have to try.*

'OK,' Tiffany said, side-glancing at Bogey then down at her still-shaking slugs.

'Right, let's go,' said Frank, trying to sound in control, though his innards felt as gooey as the floor. For the first time ever, he felt a little bit scared of his friend. And it was a horrible, confusing feeling. *Please let this work*, he thought. 'I'll tell Mum and Dad we're going out for a quick walk and that Bogey's having a lie-in.'

'GRRRRR!'

Bogey suddenly leapt towards the friends again.

'Stop that, Bogey,' cried Frank, his heart jumping into his mouth and boinging on his tongue. 'You stay here. Don't come out until we come and get you, OK?' He turned to Tiffany, trying to stop his voice wobbling and ignoring the tickles in his nose. It felt like a volcano was about to erupt in there. 'Quick – we've got an hour before the TV crew arrive. They can't see Bogey like this. **NO MATTER WHAT**.'

CHAPTER 17

RUGBY BALLS

'**W**oah!' cried Frank and Tiffany as they approached Gary Plonk's fields.

Yesterday the sweetcorn crops had been tiny. Today they were a whopping great forest, three storeys tall, with corncobs the size of rugby balls!

'What on earth—?'

'Heelloooo children!' A voice sounded from behind a tree-trunk-thick plant. Plonk stepped out looking happy as can be, despite **THE STINK**, which was even stronger here than at Snozzle Castle.

Frank and Tiffany exchanged surprised glances. Things were getting weirder by the second.

'Look at these beauties!' Plonk said, holding up a corn kernel the size of a giant gobstopper. He sounded positively giddy. 'The man said it'd work – like on his own courgettes. But mow me over with a moo-cow! I didn't think he meant the corn would grow overnight! And so big. Cor! I can hardly believe it.'

'A man? What man?' said Frank.

'Dunno. Blond quiff. Gold hoop earring. Very persuasive. Strange, really. Early yesterday morning, I'd just been thinking how my crops hadn't been doing so well, when this salesman turned up at the farm. *Got this new fertilizer*, he said. ***Boblo's Grow Pellets***. And look at this. It's a bloomin' miracle.'

He teetered for a second, looking a little bit dazed.

'Erm, Mr Plonk,' said Frank. '**THE STINK**'s really strong here. Do you know what caused it?'

'**THE STINK**? Oh, erm, nothing to do with me, I'm sure,' he said, before wandering off into his sweetcorn forest again.

OK, this was seriously strange.

Tiffany's gaze fell to the floor. 'Look,' she whispered, and pointed to some soggy blue and yellow pellets in the gaps between the ginormous plants. Parts of them had mixed to make green slime. 'What's that?'

'Not snot,' said Frank, bending down to get a better look. He recognized snot like you and me recognize a good Bally-Wally Ball.

Sammy, Violet, Peach and Slim shuddered in their jar. It reminded them of slug pellets.

'Do you think **THE STINK** might have happened when the pellets got wet?' Tiffany suggested. 'Plonk was watering his crops when we smelt it, remember?'

'Maybe,' said Frank. 'There's only one way to find out.' Checking they were out of sight from Plonk, Frank drew out his water bottle and carefully poured a few drops on to the stray pellets. Immediately, the yellow and blue mixed to make green, before fizzing and filling the air with . . . **THE STINK**!

'**GOOLIEMALOOLIE!** That's it,' said Frank. 'It's the fertilizer. Quick – we've still got time before the TV crew gets here. If we rush home now, we can jump on the computer, search for the Boblo company, call them and ask how to reverse **THE STINK** – you know, like an antidote or something.'

'Sounds like a plan,' said Tiffany, cheering up a little. And for a moment the friends forgot how scared Bogey had made them feel.

Once they'd spoken to the Boblo company, Bogey'd be back to normal, wowing the TV people before you could say *'FORGET THE REST, YOU'RE THE BEST!'*

But alas, dear stinkers . . . I mean nose-pickers . . . No, I mean stinkers who pick their noses. Frank and Tiffany couldn't have been more wrong. For they never made it back to the castle to check the computer.

What? Why?

Because the second they ran into Snozzle's grounds to take the shortcut through the outdoor stage area where they rehearsed and performed their shows for Honkerty's villagers, they ran straight into:

FERGUS THE SMELLY FIELD MOUSE!

No. No. Sorry. Fergus (fortunately) wasn't there.

No. They ran straight into BOGEY - **ANGRY, SQUIDGEPEA-OOZING, ABOUT-ANOTHER-FOOT-TALLER-THAN-EARLIER BOGEY** - who was **GOOING** and **GAAING** on his podium like an ogre gone gaga. Binky and the bats were flapping in terror, with Mum and Dad trying to calm them down.

And as if that weren't bad enough, next to them was a man with ripped jeans, looking into the viewfinder of a camera, and a woman with a gold baseball cap marked 'Producer' – both wearing nose pegs.

GOOLIEMALOOLIE! THE TV CREW WERE EARLY!

CHAPTER 18

THE SPECIAL ONE!

'**AND CUT!**' cried the director, as Frank and Tiffany arrived in panic. 'We're gonna have to do that again.' He sounded irritated as he eyed Bogey's gloopy arms swiping at the bats willy-nilly, sending snot all over the stage floor. 'We can't use any of that. We need *beautiful* bat CHOREOGRAPHY.' He sighed, adjusting his nose peg and mumbling, 'Judge Dingaling said this'd be easy!'

'Ah, children! Come and say *helloooooo!*' Mum sang with a flurry of operatic notes, before squeaking into Frank's

ear, 'Bogey came into the kitchen the second the crew arrived. I couldn't do anything except go along with it. But something's seriously wrong!' Then she smiled sweetly, and said in her normal voice, 'Frank, Tiffany, this is the director, Mike.'

Frank wanted to scream, **Noooooooooooo!** This was a disaster. But he couldn't, so he shook Mike's hand and watched in horror as Bogey sneezed so hard the bats flew away and a snot splodge landed on the camera.

'Nothing to worry about,' cried Dad, rushing over with a cloth to wipe the lens (and get a good look at the model of camera Mike was using).

Frank and Tiffany gave each other a worried stare. What on earth were they going to do?

'And this is Rita, the show's producer,' said Dad.

'Hi,' Rita said, transfixed by a proper whopper squidgepea. 'Does he always do that?'

'Erm . . .' Frank didn't know what to say.

'Well, I s'pose extra goo'll make for better TV,' Rita declared with a puzzled shrug. Then she removed her nose peg, saying, 'Bit tight, this,' and took in a deep breath through her mouth.

'Isn't this just *wonderfuuuuuuul?*' cried Mum, butting in with a high-pitched squeal.

'Oh, yes, fantastic!' Frank and Tiffany said in unison.

But this was about as wonderful as a nozz-scratch (you know, that painful moment when you scratch your own nose while going for a booger).

Frank's nose was burning so much now, it hurt. 'Tiffany,' he whispered, 'I think my tickles are telling me Bogey's getting worse. We have to get him away from here and call the Boblo company fast. Who knows what he'll do? If they keep filming him like this, we'll lose the final before we even get there. We need to stop this, now.' *And as it's my nose that's tickling*, he thought, *I'm the one to do it.*

'Erm, Mike, Rita,' Frank said, trying his best to sound like a grown-up (it felt very strange), 'Bogey's ill, I'm afraid, and needs to go back to bed. Mum, Dad, I meant to tell you earlier. He's got a cold.' Frank felt his freckly cheeks glow bright red with guilt as he purposely didn't mention the

splatted bedroom or **THE STINK** theory. 'That's why he's acting like this and sneezing and sweating squidgepeas. So he can't be in the report.'

'No can do,' said Mike. 'No offence or anything, but Judge Dingaling said Bogey's the special one.' His expression suggested he couldn't see why. Bogey was shouting '**GOO-GOO-GOOEY**' now, while stomping about the podium angrily. 'Dingaling sent the brief. Without Bogey there's no TV report.'

'What? B-but we're all good,' Mum spluttered.

'Er . . . yeah,' said Rita, moving into the audience area for a sit-down. 'But the brief's the brief. And no TV report means no final.'

GOOLIEMALOOLIE! What should they do? Frank wanted to pick his nose . . . and scream . . . and pick his nose even more.

'It won't take long,' said Mike, rubbing his nose and putting his peg in his pocket, like Rita. 'The faster we get this over with the better.' He inhaled through his mouth. 'We just need a few shots, then we'll get packin' and

your slime man can go to bed early, ready for the big day tomorrow.'

Frank looked at Bogey and watched his skin suddenly bubble with big bogey pustules. Was he growing again? **'GOOLIEMALOO–!'**

'FILM ME,' Mum interrupted, stepping forward, oblivious. 'I'll do my bit while Bogey has a break. Then everyone else can do theirs, if necessary. He might feel better in a minute.'

And before Frank could argue, Mike shrugged and cried, 'OK. Pegs off everyone. AND . . . ACTION!'

'Have you ever had a tickle in your nose . . .'

. . . Mum began. It was from the song 'A-Choooo', her sure-fire hit from their first ever show.

'It gets you from your head down to your toes.

Then there's nothing left to do,

But let out a sneezy, snotty, sloppy, sticky A-ch—'

But suddenly, terrifyingly – just as she hit her high 'A-choooo' note, **THE STINK** got worse.

And then (prepare yourselves, stinkers), the unthinkable happened.

CHAPTER 19

POOT PANDEMIC

Mum let out the biggest, squidgyest, most gurgling fart her body had ever created!

PFFFFFFFFFFFFFFFFFFFFFFFFFFFFF FFFFFFFF-SCHULG-ULG-ULG!

Mum turned beetroot red.

Mike and Rita looked shocked.

Frank, Tiffany and Dad gulped.

Then slowly, horrifyingly, one by one, everybody started:

PARP! went Dad.

PROUT! went Mike.

TOOT, TOOT, TOOT, TOOT! went Sammy, Violet, Peach and Slim.

PFFFFFFFFFFFFFFFFFFF! went Rita, so hard her bottom actually lifted off her seat.

WHOOOOOFFFFF-PROOOOOOT! went Frank and Tiffany at the same time.

SPLOOF! went Bogey.

It was a proper poot pandemic!

And it didn't just stay in Snozzle Castle either. Over in the village, people had started to bum-pop too.

'Excuse me!' cried Mrs Wirrel as her botty-burp caused her poodles' coats to ripple.

'Great gherkins!' shouted Walter Wills as his whiffy-whoops blew over a pile of apples.

'Nooooooo!' cried Bo Jacobs as he accidentally farted Squishy up on to the roof of his bungalow, where she fell into the drainpipe, and whooshed straight back down.

'Yikes!' yelled Mrs Sniff as her mega-trump blew Clawdia out through the cat flap.

'Cockadoodle!' screamed Farmer Plonk as his fluffadora blew some whopper corn kernels into the air.

For yes, stinkers, gas-blasting or butt-bassooning or whoosh-hurdling or trouser-trumpeteering or popping-a-fluffy – or whatever you like to call it (you choose) — was the side effect **THE STINK** had on humans (and on Bogey too, it would seem), and the one I warned you about at the beginning of this book!

Back at Snozzle Castle, Frank screamed to Tiffany, 'This has to be **THE STINK**'s doing!'

THRRRRP!

But she couldn't answer, 'cause there, suddenly, towering above them was Bogey, growling a deep rumble that sounded like thunder . . .

'Grrrr! Grrrr! GrrrrRRRRRRRRRRRRRRR!'

'ARGHHHHH!' Tiffany and Frank screamed in unison.

And then, as a breeze blew another wave of the hideous Stink towards them all, Bogey let out a master-blaster – BLARP – and started to change . . .

One step . . .

His gloopy arms and legs swelled to five, ten . . . FIFTY times their normal size as every goodie cell in his body morphed into a nasty wobbler and multiplied!

Two steps . . .

His gooey, pustule-ridden body BALLOONED to the size of a block of flats.

Three steps . . .

His massive nose started sneezing GIGANTIC snot ABSOLUTELY EVERYWHERE!

'FLY AWAAAAAAAAAAAAAAY!' screamed Binky the bat in terror (which really sounded like '*SQUEAKSQUEEEEEEEEEEEAK!*').

For – oh, divert your eyes, stinkers – Bogey was an angry, sixty-foot tall goo-dripping MONSTER!

GRRRRRRRR!

DANGER ALERT!
DANGER ALERT!

'A-GHOOOOOOO!'
SPLAT!

Did you hear that, stinkers?

SPLOTCH!
SPLAT!
SPLOTCH!

'Tis the terrible sound of Monster Bogey's enormous sneezes flying out his nose and hitting the ground with a G-force of 214 (that's Goo-force, not Gravitational-force). Oh, and there goes another! **SPLAT!** And another. **SPLOTCH!** And another. **SPLAT!**

SPLOTCH! SPLAT!
SPLAT! SPLOTCH!
SPLAT! SPLAT! SPLAT!

QUICK! HIDE UNDER A TABLE!
OR UNDER YOUR BED.
OR EVEN UNDER YOUR LITTLE BROTHER
OR SISTER IF YOU'VE GOT ONE.
'CAUSE BOGEY'S ON THE RAMPAGE!!!!!!!!!!!!
AND THINGS ARE ABOUT TO GET EVEN
STICKIER!

CHAPTER 20

I-I CAN'T!

'**G**OOOOO-GOOOOO-GOOOOOEY!'

Bogey's ginormous angry body shot up towards the sky, his arms outstretched like a gargantuan zombie.

'**ARE YOU GETTING THIIIIS?**' screamed Rita, recording the scene on her phone from under her chair.

'**YEEEEEEES!**' screamed Mike from the stage, pointing his camera straight at Bogey's contorted face until – '**A-A-GHOOOOO! A-A-GHOOOOO! A-A-GHOOOOO!**'– a succession of sneezes whooshed out of Bogey's giant nose

like demonic rain, pinning Mike to the floor.

Everyone was in danger.

'TAKE COVER!' screamed Frank.

But that was easier said than done. Bogey had just leapt off his podium with a whopper popper.

BOOM!
SPLAT!
POP!

And he was heading towards ...

'Tiffany! LOOK OUT!' Frank rushed over and pushed her and the slugs out of the way, a mere second before Bogey's foot slammed down on the seat she'd been hiding under.

'You all OK?' asked Frank, panting.

'I-I think so,' she replied (checking on the slugs and letting out a windy-squish of her own). But really, Frank knew she wasn't. And as Bogey's gargantuan, dripping body trampled past, showering her and Frank with goop, that same feeling of terror and confusion he'd felt in Bogey's room suddenly whooshed back into his toes and multiplied by a million-zillion. And he could see Tiffany felt the same.

'What are we going to do?' Frank cried.

'I don't know,' she said, trembling. She clutched the slug jar for comfort (though Sammy, Violet, Peach and Slim were wobbling too).

'We need a plan,' cried Frank.

'I-I can't . . .' said Tiffany.

'OK, I'll try and think of one,' said Frank.

'No. I-I mean I can't . . . help!' Tiffany blurted. She didn't know how she was going to say this. 'Frank –' a tear rolled down her cheek – 'I don't think Bogey's the friend we know any more.'

Frank looked up to see Bogey ripping off the stage curtain.

'He's changed. He's a . . .' She winced as she said it. 'A monster. A real monster.'

The words struck Frank's heart like an axe. He couldn't believe Tiffany would even think such a thing.

'B-but none of this is his fault,' he stuttered. 'It's **THE STINK**. You saw that. No matter how angry and scary he gets, he needs us, remember? It's what friends do! He's still our friend!'

'I-I'm sorry,' said Tiffany, her eyes wide with terror. 'I'm too scared.' And she rushed off through the goop, dodging sneezes and broken bits of theatre, desperate to get to safety in the castle.

Frank felt as though the world had come crashing down around him. And as the ripped theatre curtain landed in a ball just metres away, he realized that it probably had.

'Tiffany!' he cried after her. He hadn't felt this sad, since . . . erm, never. How could she do this to him? To Bogey?

'GRRRRRRRRRRRRRRRR!'

There was no time to dwell on it . . .

Bogey had changed course and was now heading towards the moat, crushing all the stage lighting under his gloopy toes. If Frank was going to help him, he had to act fast.

'I'm coming, Bogey,' Frank cried, pushing all thoughts

of Tiffany aside and trying not to blub.

Then, inadvertently filling his trousers with yet more bum gas, he squelched his way quickly towards his monster friend, dodging sneeze splats as he went, before taking shelter behind the garden shed.

Now what?

Emotions were whooshing round his brain: **DISTRESS** that Tiffany had left him. **FEAR** because Bogey had become huge and dangerous. **TERROR** that Bogey would hurt himself or somebody else. And **WORRY** that someone might try to stop Bogey by ki— He couldn't bear finishing that thought . . .

DISTRESS . . .

FEAR   **TERROR**

WORRY   **WHOOSH!**   **DISTRESS**

FEAR   **TERROR**

WORRY   **DISTRESS**

FEAR

He had to do something!!!!!

He looked up at Bogey's contorted face. His peggy teeth were like brick walls, his tongue was lolloping out of his mouth like a devilish funfair slide and his sneezes were beyond anything Frank had ever seen. But they weren't the most dangerous thing – yet. The most dangerous thing right now was him walking, crushing everything in his path and causing the snot on the ground to swell and churn.

If Frank could stop Bogey from moving, he might just be able to stop the destruction and make sure everyone was safe. And then he'd help Bogey by . . . well, he'd work that out later.

CHAPTER 21

DON'T LOOK DOWN

Right, here's another quiz.

QUESTION 1: *How do you stop a sixty-foot Bogey Monster all alone without your best friend?*

☐ **A. By shouting, 'Oy you! Want a banana?'**

☐ **B. By dancing a jig in pointy shoes with little bells on the end.**

☐ **C. You don't have a dingley-wingley of an idea, but talking to him might be a good start.**

If you answered C, then you're just like Frank.

The problem was that between the noisy farting, the loud sneezing and the large distance between Frank's mouth and Bogey's ears, being heard was going to be hard.

And so he needed to get up high, close to Bogey's earhole.

But how? He looked around him and Snozzle Castle gave him the answer.

Stinkers, **NEVER EVER EVER** do this at home.

Climbing a castle tower, all alone, without your best friend and without safety equipment, is **VERY DANGEROUS**.

No. Worse.

It's **DANGEROUSOUSOUSOUS**, which is the worst, longest kind of danger there is.

If you ever have to choose between doing this and nibbling green-tinted Bikkie-Wikkies on the loo, choose the bikkies. You might get crumbs in your pants or accidentally drop a bite into the bowl, but at least you won't have to climb uneven ancient brick covered in slippery slime and risk falling to your death.

Frank didn't have that choice. He didn't have any Bikkie-Wikkies. Plus, his friend was getting ever closer to the tower, which meant he had to climb it. NOW! So, with his hands a-shaking and his tootles a-tootling, he slowly, carefully started the ascent.

One stick-outy stone ...

All good so far, he thought.

Five stick-outy stones ...

Still OK.

Ten stick-outy stones ...

Hmm, this is getting high. If only Tiffany were with me.

His stomach clenched as he quickly looked around for her, but she was nowhere to be seen. She had let him down, but he hoped she and the slugs were safe.

Fifteen stick-outy stones ...

GLUPS! He half-wished Mum and Dad would spot him now and tell him to stop. But when

he saw them (up to their knees in goop, talking agitatedly with Mike and Rita), they weren't looking his way, so he carried on.

Twenty stick-outy stones . . .

GOOLIEMALOOLIE! DON'T LOOK DOWN!

Two hundred and fifty stick-outy stones . . .

URGH! These ones were **COVERED IN GIANT SNEEZES.**

Taking extra care, he shakily placed each hand and foot on a slimy brick, but . . .

. . . **WHEEEEEP!**

A whopper blast escaped his bum, setting him off balance, and – 'Argh!' – his hand glided off the brick and . . .

'OOF!' He caught himself just in time on a groove a few centimetres below.

(What did I tell you, stinkers? One nanosecond more, and he would have plunged to the ground and certain death. Always choose the Bikkie-Wikkies!)

Then, with his heart beating a gazillion miles an hour,

he reached the turret directly above Bogey's head.

'Bogey, stop moving!' he tried calling, but his friend just stomped forward, arms outstretched, and couldn't hear him.

He needed to get nearer.

He needed to jump, now!

CHAPTER 22

OOZING LAGOONS!

After three, stinkers.

ONE

TWO

THREE!

. . . with a quick glance down, Frank leapt off the tower and straight onto Bogey's squelchy head.

SPLATCH!

'GRRRRRR!'

Bogey thrashed and growled. Squidgepeas flew off in every direction.

Frank lay flat and clung on. **'SSHHHHHHHHHH, IT'S OK, BOGEY,'** he shouted. **'IT'S ME, FRANK! YOU NEED TO STAY STILL! EVERYTHING WILL BE FINE.'**

But things weren't fine. Suddenly, with his monstrous arms outstretched like a gooey sleepwalker, Bogey started moving again.

BOOM-SPLAT!
BOOM-SPLAT!
BOOM!

'STOP, BOGEY!' Frank screeched, trying not to slip off.

But Bogey continued – through Snozzle Castle garden, over the gates and on into Honkerty Village, where it was a . . .

'HELP!' 'HELP!' HERE
AND A SCREAM 'HELP!' THERE,
HERE A 'HELP!', THERE A 'HELP!'
EVERYWHERE A SCREAM 'HELP!'

. . . as Bogey's ginormous body slopped its way down Honkerty-Honk-Honk, Hooter Alley, Sneaky Beak Lane and Snout Back Alley, sneezing hundreds – no, thousands

– no, millions of snottywotties (the official name for what came out of Bogey's nose) on to the pavement to form whopper puddles, which globbed together to form thick, oozing lagoons, which merged to form tides of goop, which suddenly whooshed towards the flatulent villagers in **a wall of thick, green waves.**

'**GRRRRR,**' growled Bogey.

'**AAAAAAHHHHHH!**' screamed Mrs Wirrel, Bo Jacobs, Mrs Sniff, Walter Wills and dozens of other people as the goop careered towards them ahead of Bogey.

'**RUN!**' Frank screamed at the top of his lungs. '**GET INDOORS!** *QUIIIICK!*'

And humans weren't the only ones in trouble.

'**HELP!**' cried Honkerty's weird hedgehog as he fell into a whirlpool of goop in front of Honkerty Library.

'**MEEEOOOOOW!**' squealed Clawdia, Mrs Sniff's cat, as she went under.

And **OH MY GOODNESS, LOOK!** The undulations of snot are rippling and churning and careering towards the edge of this page too!

QUICK! YOU'RE
IN DANGER!
FIND A BOOKMARK,
SHUT THE BOOK
QUICKLY AND
COUNT TO TEN.
THEN OPEN IT!

CHAPTER 23

CATASTROPHE!

You're back. It worked! Goodness me. That was close.

Now, where were we?

Yes, we're back in Honkerty, where . . .

'**GOOLIEMALOOLIE, NO!**' Frank couldn't believe it. There, hacking through the sky towards them in a swirl of lights and blades like a demonic dragonfly, was a **HELICOPTER!**, The police were here!

'**STAY WHERE YOU ARE!**' came a megaphoned voice from the copter. '**I REPEAT. DON'T MOVE.**'

The helicopter was approaching fast now, and Frank

could see it had a gigantic net suspended from it.

'**KEEP GOING!**' cried Frank to Bogey, panicking. If the police caught his monster friend, goodness knows what'd happen to him. He needed to get Bogey to shelter somewhere, to buy them more time and think of a plan – and perhaps even explain that this was all just a Stink-related misunderstanding. ***BUT WHERE?***

He looked around him.

HELP! There was nowhere to go.

And to Frank's horror, a second later the helicopter was above them, the downwash from its powerful blades spraying goop everywhere. It was all Frank could do to stay on Bogey's head.

Shielding his eyes, Frank dared to look up for a split second, and as he did, he saw the words **SNOTLAND YARD** written on the helicopter, and a policeman with a blond moustache and a hoop earring hanging out of its door.

'Hand him over!' the policeman shouted.

'**NO!**' Frank cried.

But before he knew it, the net was loose and tumbling

straight towards them.

The mesh landed on Bogey in a whirl of cord and snot, and he flailed and growled and bit and kicked.

'GRRRRRRRRRRRRRRRRR!'

But still the helicopter lifted him upwards.

SCHLUUUUCK! ('Twas the sound of his gargantuan feet being slurped out of the goo below.)

'GRRRR!'

Then, as Bogey rose into the air, thrashing and bashing and fighting against the net, Frank found himself sliding off Bogey's head, down his body and on to his leg, where he hung on for dear life.

'Help! Tiffany!' he shouted, forgetting for a split second that, for the first time ever, she wasn't there.

Within seconds, the helicopter was rising fast and Frank was struggling to keep his grip.

And then, catastrophe!

He farted for the one-hundred-and-twenty-seventh time since this whole nightmare had begun, and slipped ...

'Woah!'

And then, as he stared at the goop rolling and tossing about the streets way below his legs, he felt his head spin and his fingers slide and – **'GLUPS!'** – Frank hurtled through the air towards the flooded ground.

The End

Oh, sorry, stinkers. That's not right.

There's definitely more . . .

Quick, turn the page.

CHAPTER 24

ASSAPANICK!

• If you think Frank splatted straight into the gloop below and drowned, raise your hand or your left ear or your right eyebrow.

• If you think a giant ladybird swooped in to save him, carried him on her back over Snozzle Castle and across hundreds of miles of countryside to drop him on to a ferry bound for Greenland, please do a handstand.

or

• If you think it was neither of those things and that the next thing Frank knew was that he was home, shout

ASSAPANICK (which isn't rude, or about flustered bottoms or anything like that; it's a name for a flying squirrel).

Well, I hope you shouted assapanick, 'cause that's exactly what happened.

'SORRY, SORRY . . .'

'Uh?' A familiar voice floated into Frank's ears as he sat up in bed. 'Tiffany?' he asked groggily. 'OOF!'

He felt himself fall back into his pillow as she flung her arms around him, crying, 'I'm just **SO SORRY**. I should have been there for you!'

The slugs backflipped on to his shoulder.

'Wha—? Wher—?' There was a buzzing in his ears. Frank was a little confused as he tried to remember what had happened. He remembered goop and falling and—

'Oh, you're awake, sweetheart,' squealed Mum, rushing

across Frank's room to kiss his cheek, avoiding the bump on his forehead. She was so distressed, she couldn't even sing her words out. 'You hit your head in the gloop and knocked yourself out. If Tiffany hadn't dived in after you . . .' She looked over at her gratefully.

Tiffany looked at her still-sticky shoes.

'I-I . . .' She took a deep breath. 'I'm just **SO SORRY**. I followed you into the village. 'Cause Frank, you're right. Friends stick together,' she said. 'Even when things get bad. I was just so . . .'

Frank didn't need her to finish. He knew she was going to say 'scared'. That was the good thing about best friends. You didn't have to say the words for the other person to understand.

'It's OK,' he said. She'd come back for him *and* saved him. 'You're my best friend, Tiffany, and you always will be. You're brilliant!'

Tiffany looked at her shoes again.

Frank's cheeks turned very pink.

They'd never had to make up like this before – and

especially not in front of their families.

'You gave us a fright,' said Dad, rushing over to hug him too. Tiffany's mum and dad were standing behind him smiling. And Binky was fluttering in front of the drawn curtains as the first light of dawn slid through the gaps.

Wait! Dawn? Frank jumped up. Where had the rest of the day and the night gone?

'**GOOLIEMALOOLIE!**' It all came flooding back. 'Where's Bogey? We've got to save Bogey!'

Mum gave him another hug. 'Oh, Frank. He's gone.' Then she let out a sudden, loud and theatrical sob. 'He was just so dangerous!'

Frank's heart dropped into his socks. He had to set things straight.

He looked at Tiffany.

If they were going to save Bogey, they had to tell their parents everything they knew.

'Did you say anything?'

'No,' she whispered. 'I was too worried about you.'

Frank nodded.

He didn't care if Mum and Dad or Tiffany's parents were angry with them, now.

'We're sorry,' he said. 'We should have told you before, but we were all so worried about what to perform for the final . . .' His stomach knotted as he thought about how they were no longer going to Warble-Blob (who'd let them perform ever again after this?). 'We didn't want to bother you. But it's **THE STINK**'s fault. We think it made Bogey go doolally. And made all of us fart. And we think it was caused by Farmer Plonk's fertilizer pellets. We first noticed the smell while we were at his field. And his crops have grown really big, just like Bogey. And when we poured water on the pellets, we smelt **THE STINK**.'

'Fertilizer pellets?' said Dad.

'Oh, my love. I think you hit your head harder than we thought,' said Mum. 'I'm pretty sure it was just the sewers. Dad checked the pipe earlier and it seemed OK. It must have unblocked itself, so that's probably why the smell's gone.'

Frank took a deep breath. **GOOLIEMALOOLIE**. The air *was*

back to normal! But his ears were still buzzing . . .

'And I've never heard of fertilizer making things grow as tall as buildings or causing wind,' Mum continued. 'Plonk's just a very good farmer, that's all.'

'Maybe Bogey was always going to grow?' Dad added. 'Maybe he was programmed for this to happen. Maybe it's best that he's gone!'

'Wha—?' How could Mum and Dad say that?

Tiffany knew. It was because his parents were scared – just like she'd been. (That's right, stinkers, grown-ups get scared too.)

'Bogey would never do anything like this on his own,' Frank shouted angrily. 'We all need to go out and look for him **NOW!** He needs our help.'

'Erm, you're not going anywhere,' said Dad, striding over to Frank's bedroom window and opening the curtain. 'None of us are.'

Frank gasped. That's where the buzzing was coming from. Not his ears, but outside! He couldn't believe it. Thousands of onlookers, TV crews (probably including

Mike and Rita) and news reporters were all lined up in front of Snozzle Castle, either interviewing the villagers, filming the weird brownish light of the snotty streets at dawn (orange light mixed with green goo creates a strange brown glow, you know) or clinging to the metal gates to film the castle.

'They've been there all night,' said Dad with a sigh.

'It seems,' said Tiffany, 'that having a **_FORGET THE REST, YOU'RE THE BEST_** star turn into a sixty-foot dripping monster makes you famous ... for all the wrong reasons. Frank ... erm ...' She took a deep breath. **'BOGEY'S GONE VIRAL!'**

CHAPTER 25

'RUN! . . . GET INDOORS! QUIIIICK!'

Frank's eyes popped right out their sockets!

No, sorry. This isn't *that* kind of book. But he did open his eyes wide and feel them bulge, 'cause Tiffany's phone showed not one, not two, not twenty, not fifty-five, but (after a long flick through) more than seventy-two videos (seventy-three, actually) of giant Bogey slopping through the village, with – **'OH NO!'** – Frank on his head, shouting, **'RUN! . . . GET INDOORS!**

QUIIIICK!'

And each video had millions of shares.

'We've lost everything.' Mum started sobbing as Tiffany's mum tried to comfort her.

'Some of the things they've been saying about us – about you, Frank – are, well, horrible,' said Dad, with a sigh. He looked ready to cry too. 'The stuff Mike and Rita recorded! Even Dicky Dingaling's had a go.'

Want to see, stinkers?

There were millions of statements, but these are five of the worst 'cause they were from people the Snozzlers knew and who had (not two days before) said they were fans. And I must warn you, they're not nice comments. Internet ones rarely are.

Mrs Sniff: I can't believe my neighbours have done this to us. They seemed so pleasant, but really, they've been harbouring . . . a MONSTER.

Mrs Wirrel: That monster's a DANGER TO SOCIETY. It's

WILD, I say. I saw the boy riding on its head. The entire family should be locked up!

Bo Jacobs: I used to love 'em. But now I don't. And nor does Squishy. They're dangerous!

Walter Wills: I'll throw rotten tomatoes at them next time I see them. I can't believe what they've done to our wonderful village. They should be punished.

Judge Dicky Dingaling: I've disqualified the Snozzlers from the *Forget the Rest, You're the Best* final tonight. It's a DISGRACE! We were duped!

As Frank read, he felt a bubble of anger fizzle in his toes, career up his legs and flip-flop on his chest. He wanted to shout and pick his nose . . . and shout and pick his nose non-stop. This was so unfair. None of this was his or Bogey's fault.

This was **THE STINK**'s doing.

And he was going to find out who was behind it.

'Tiffany?' he whispered as soon as their parents had left the room to grab a cup of tea. Binky fluttered on to Frank's shoulder to listen. 'Mum and Dad don't believe us, so we need to do something about this ourselves. Did you manage to find out anything about Boblo's Grow Pellets?'

'No. I searched while you were asleep, but there's nothing.' (It's true, stinkers, if you check the internet with a grown-up now, you'll find absolutely zip.)

'Well, first things first. We need to find Bogey and somehow reverse **THE STINK**'s effect, then bring him back to safety. *Then* we need to prove that this was all **THE STINK**'s doing.' Frank didn't have the foggiest how they'd do any of this, but this was the plan and he was sticking with it. 'Something tells me we'll find out about this Boblo thing while we're at it. And I don't think it was the real police who took him.'

'But how are we going to find Bogey?' said Tiffany. 'He could be anywhere by now.'

Frank twitched the curtains and looked at the masses

outside. Beyond the reporters at the gates, some people had put on their wellies and started cleaning up the goo with hosepipes.

'Tiffany!' he suddenly gasped. Gosh, it felt good to be friends again. 'I've got an idea.'

CHAPTER 26

SNOT! SNOT! SNOT!
SNOT! SNOT! SNOT!
SNOT! SNOT! SNOT!

Can you guess what that idea might be, stinkers?

The clue's in the chapter title.

But, here, I'll let Frank say it.

'**SNOT!**' he blurted. 'Bogey was still dripping and sneezing when they took him, so there must be a trail of whopper goo we can follow, between the village and wherever he's been taken! I just hope it's not too far away!'

'Yes, of course!' said Tiffany. 'But we'll have to sneak out without being seen.'

'MEEP!' went the slugs (which meant, 'Great idea! We'll come!').

FLAP, FLAP, went Binky (which meant, 'And you're not going without me!').

Tiffany walked over to Frank's secret cupboard door and opened its back panel. It led to a hidden passage through the castle walls and the dungeon, and out into the back garden by the moat. Frank's mum and dad had never found out about it, even during the castle's renovations, so the friends often used it to sneak out and play.

'Once we're in the garden,' she said, 'we can grab our bikes from the garage. I don't think the goo's as deep there. Then we can push through the bushes, where no one will notice.'

'It's a plan!' said Frank, then froze. 'Listen!'

Their parents' voices were sailing down the corridor towards his room.

'Quick!' Tiffany said. 'We need to help Bogey now – EVEN if it gets scary. Let's go, before they see us.'

CHAPTER 26 ½

ARE YOU WORRIED, STINKERS?

I AM. AND YOU SHOULD BE TOO.

'CAUSE IF YOU THINK ALL THIS 'GOING VIRAL' STUFF'S BAD FOR THE SNOZZLERS RIGHT NOW, IT'S NOTHING COMPARED TO WHAT'S BEEN HAPPENING TO BOGEY.

WANNA KNOW WHAT THAT IS?

WELL, PRESS THIS TIME-TRAVEL DOT AND YOU'LL FIND OUT (THOUGH YOU SHOULD PROBABLY COVER YOUR EYES).

Oh, sorry, wrong one. Try this one . . .

Drataloo! Wrong again. This one . . . ?

That's better.

CHAPTER 27

TAKE THAT!

Well done. You've just travelled fourteen hours back in time to the moment when the helicopter (with Bogey in the net below) was hovering over the helipad of the **LAB RATS'** top-secret bunker.

'We're in position,' shouted Lobbo through his megaphone, leaning over the edge of the chopper's door. 'Daphne, open the roof.'

With a loud **SWISH**, the helipad split into two to reveal a huge, brightly lit, all-white chamber below, with nothing

but a huge laser gun in the corner, a mesh cage, Lobbo's computer, a lab table, an 'Emergency Self-Destruct' button on the wall (like in every room; in case anyone ever tried to steal Lobbo's technology) and a glass wall overlooking the gigantic courgette garden.

'Lower him in slowly,' shouted Lobbo. 'I don't want more goo than necessary in my lab. I knew he'd grow, but he's bigger than even I could have imagined. I've outdone myself with the **STINKUS-DINKUS-INUS-NOZZLEUS-HORRIBLIS** this time.'

Lil Hunk pressed a button on the copter's control panel, and the net was lowered to the floor of the lab.

'Bendy, you keep an eye on him, we'll be there in a mo,' Lobbo shouted, as the helipad began to close over Bendy's head.

'OK boss,' she said, using her flexy, acrobatic muscles to shimmy down the rope, then jump into the chamber next to Bogey's huge, thrashing body.

'Now, now, now,' said Lobbo, striding into the room with Daphne and Lil Hunk moments later.

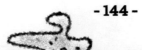

(Wondering how they'd got in from the helipad, stinkers? With another secret rock, of course; though this rock wasn't on the ground outside. It was on the roof, and opened a secret lift straight into the lab.)

The Rats were dwarfed by Bogey's giant pink tongue, which was lolloping through the holes in the net as he growled and kicked his legs, but they weren't scared. Lobbo was too good at keeping things under control.

'Ha! He's quite hideous, isn't he?' Lobbo cried.

The **LAB RATS** all sniggered.

'Now, what are we going to do with you? You're such a whopping weapon of chaos, it almost seems a shame to turn you back.' He sighed. 'But I've tried out my Stink, so now I need to try out the antidote. Plus, I can't keep you here if you're big enough to eat me. No. I'll shrink you down, while my genius mind works out what to do with you next.'

He pointed at Lil Hunk, who immediately dragged over the laser gun. 'I call this device the "Anti-Stink". Now, HOLD STILL!' he cried nastily, sensing all the jealosity he'd ever felt towards Bogey suddenly rush up his body and into his blond quiff, where it rustled for a moment, before cascading down on to his face to form the biggest wicksmirk he'd ever wicksmirked.

CRZZZZZZZZZZZZZZZZZZZZZZZZZZZZ

'**TAKE THAT!** You bat genius,' Lobbo shrieked, as he pushed the button to activate the machine.

The Anti-Stink beam hit Bogey straight between his eyes, immediately turning all his wobbler cells back into goodies – SLOOP! – which turned his body straight back to its normal size.

And then Bogey started to shake with fear, as the memory of everything that had happened – his angriness, the snotting of his bedroom, his growling at the moon, his morphing into a sixty-foot mucus machine that got bogeynapped by the chopper – came flooding back in one giant memory ball. And then he wanted to run. And hide. But the net was too heavy for him to escape from, and – quite frankly, after so much stress – he was feeling as limp as a soggy tissue.

'Ooh, ooh, ooooooh,' shouted Lobbo excitedly, as he strutted around Bogey's now normal-sized body. 'It worked. I've done it! I've turned you back.' He did a little pirouette. 'There was always a chance you'd frazzle. And goodness knows what it'd do to humans! I mean, what's the opposite of letting out a fart? Filling up with air? Ha! Who cares? You're not human, so here you are!' And then he turned to the *LAB RATS* and cried, 'Of course I've done it. I AM A GENIUS!'

'You are!' cried Daphne, with a proud nod.

'Yeah!' cried Lil Hunk.

'Yeah!' cried Bendy, doing the splits like a cheerleader.

'Show off!' huffed Daphne.

'Leave her alone,' said Lil Hunk.

'Or what?' Daphne looked him straight in his bloodshot eyes.

'I'll break your guitar!'

'You wouldn't.'

'Try me!'

'**LAB RATS, LAB RATS**. Not in front of our guest,' Lobbo smirked. 'But I see you're in high spirits, which is good, because now that we've eliminated the Snozzlers from the competition, just as I said we'd do, tonight's **FORGET THE REST, YOU'RE THE BEST** is ours for the taking . . . so let's take it!'

'YEAH!' cried the **LAB RATS** in harmony (immediately forgetting their squabble). Daphne was on D, Bendy was on F sharp and Lil Hunk was on an A.

Then Lobbo joined in with a low D and sang, '*Lil Hunk and Bendy, get this goo cleaned up, will you? And Daphne, throw this monstrosity in here.*' He tapped the mesh cage

and changed to a high D. *'We'll keep him here 'til after the show. Then I'll experiment on him. He'll be my post-win reward!'* Then his voice went especially deep and gravelly as an idea came. 'We could even see if we can make him into one of **LOBBO'S LAB RATS**! HA! See you later, loser!'

CHAPTER 28

A-A-GHOOOOOOOOOO!
A-A-GHOOOOOOOOOO!
A-A-GHOOOOOOOOOO!

Now, stinky-winks, if Lobbo and his rotten lot hadn't been so full of themselves, and their dastardly crimes and their bickering and their amazing harmonies, they might have noticed the beginnings of what you're about to see and might never have left the lab.

But pride stints your thinks (I mean, your 'thinkings'... no, I mean, your 'thoughts'), so they missed what happened (while they were perfecting their new bike balancing act),

which means you stinkers are the only people in the entire world who will ever really know the truth about this next bit.

Ready?

You might want to grab a pack of tissues and a couple of calming green Bikkie-Wikkies, 'cause it's gonna get sticky and, well . . . you'll see. (Need to make the biscuits? The recipe's on page 245. I know. My pleasure.)

Alone, slumped on the floor of the cage, Bogey felt sad. Sadder than sad. Not only was he trapped, he was also heartbroken and stricken with guilt as he thought of his friends and family and all the terrible things he'd done to them – like growling . . . and flicking chumpclumps . . . and nearly crushing them with his bus-sized feet while trampling their performance venue! 'GOO-GA-GORRY,' he murmured to himself, which meant, 'Frank and Tiffany, I'm so sorry!'

And then, as if that weren't enough, his body started to feel strange, as if every part of him was jiggling around

inside.

And that's because it was! Here, press this snot ball and I'll show you:

Look. It's all his cells bumping and bashing into each other.

Why?

Because **THE STINK** had made his goodie cells change into wobblers, which had multiplied (which is why he'd grown). And now the Anti-Stink had shrunk him back to normal size, his extra cells – all goodies now, thank goodness – had nowhere to go, so they were fighting to get out.

'GAAAAAA!'

It was making his legs wobble and his arms jiggle and his nose tickle and . . .

**'A-A-GHOOOOOOOOOO!
A-A-GHOOOOOOOOOO!
A-A-GHOOOOOOOOOO!'**

Three ENORMOUS sneezes whizzed through the mesh

of the cage and landed on the lab floor!

Bogey's body felt calmer after that, but not his emotions, for as he stared at the globs on the floor, it reminded him of all the flooding he'd caused in Honkerty Village and of Frank and Tiffany, and all the people and animals he'd put in danger, and that made him cry.

And as he did, three Anti-Stink tears rolled down his bumpy cheeks and on to the lab floor. One tear for each glob.

And as the tears hit the sneeze globs, little sparks leapt into the air.

And then the globs started to move. And multiply. And make little squelchy sounds. And clump together to form bigger globs, which then – much to Bogey's astonishment – started hopping up one on top of the other to mush together to form **NOT ONE, NOT TWO**, but **THREE** little **bogey monsters!** Just like him.

And within seconds, they were perfect. His mirror image. Only a quarter of his height, with green eyes and slightly flatter heads!

And as they stood there, wobbling on their bobbly legs beyond the cage, making cute little **GAA-GOO** noises (in surprisingly harmonious ways), Bogey, who was trembling from head to webbed toe in shock, cried **'GOO-GOO-GOOOOOOOOEY!'** which meant, **'STICKY SNOT BALLS! I'M A DAD!'**

Because yes, dearest stinkers, that's exactly what he'd just become.

CHAPTER 29

PRIVATE PROPERTY – KEEP OUT OR DIE WOOD

'**I** don't like this,' said Frank, peering into the darkness over his handlebars at a sign marked:

~~FLUFFY FAIRY WOOD~~ **PRIVATE PROPERTY – KEEP OUT OR DIE WOOD**

'Nor me,' Tiffany whispered, getting off her bike for a stretch. They'd pedalled hard all morning and her legs were on fire. 'It looks very spooky.' She popped a few leaves into the slugs' jar for their breakfast. 'But this is where the snots lead.'

Frank looked up past Binky, who was flapping overhead, and saw some goo dripping from the treetops. The air smelt damp, like rotting wood. And as Tiffany got out her phone and shone the torch into the trees, they saw huge spiderwebs glistening between pointy bushes like humungous nets and – **GOOLIEMALOOLIE** – was that a mouse crossed with a hippo?

'Tiffany. There's a path over there,' Frank suddenly whispered.

'It looks well creepy. And dangerous. You sure we should go?'

'N-No,' Frank gulped. 'But Bogey needs us. Come on.' He pulled at a gap in the bushes and – leaving their bikes behind – they clambered through.

It *was* well creepy in the woods. Webs hung like traps, gnarly tree roots made them trip and eerie 'OOOOOs' filled the air like a crowd of ghoulish owls. Even Binky seemed spooked, flapping down to grip on to Frank's shoulder.

Then, just as the friends thought the dark twists and turns would never end, the pale haze of morning began

to dapple through the thinning canopies and the smell of rotting wood morphed into the aroma of new grass and fresh mushrooms, and they found themselves in a clearing, where –

'**GOOLIEMALOOLIE,**' whispered Frank.

'SOARING SLUGS!'

'MEEP!'

'EEK!'

– there was the biggest, most state-of-the-art bunker they'd ever ogled – all grand and flat, with slick concrete walls and a helipad topped with a police chopper marked '**SNOTLAND YARD**'!

Tiffany gasped.

'Look! It's the fake police helicopter. Bogey has to be inside that building!' Frank whispered, not knowing whether to rejoice or cry. 'We've got to find a way in. Come on.'

Then he touched his nose gently and said, 'Hold tight, Bogey, we're on our way!'

CHAPTER 30

AFTER-SHOW TREAT!

Frank, Tiffany and the slugs weren't the only people who were on their way.

After a very long and particularly energetic new dance routine, the **LAB RATS** were heading back to the lab, dabbing their sweaty brows and laughing at their own cleverness, ready to check on . . . ehem . . . have a go at Bogey, 'cause, well, it was the first time Lobbo had used the Anti-Stink laser, and a good scientist always checks his subjects . . . ehem . . . victims. Plus, he wanted a good old gloat.

'Fame, Fame, Fame,
The world will know our name.
We're gonna win the show today,
Fame, Fame Fame,'

they sang loudly as they opened the lab door and entered the room, still full of their own brilliance.

'Er, shouldn't that be, "Fame, Fame, Fame. It's thanks to the Snozzlers"?' said Bendy suddenly. "Cause it is kind of thanks to them we're through?'

Lobbo turned red. There'd been nothing but silly questions all through rehearsals. 'No. It's thanks to MY genius that we're through,' he snapped. 'And anyway, "fame" doesn't rhyme with "Snozzlers", does it? It rhymes with "nam—"'

He stopped in his tracks. **GLUPS!**

Daphne stopped in her tracks. **GLUPS!**

Bendy and Lil Hunk stopped in their tracks: **GLUPS! GLUPS!**

For there, clinging to Bogey's cage, wobbling like jelly and blowing weird raspberries at the sight of the **LAB RATS**, were (as you well know) **THREE flat-headed bogey babies**. And the sight was (as you can imagine) surprising. How surprising?

Grab a calculator.

Type 6,000,000 (that's six million). Then subtract 5,941,924. Hit equals. Turn it upside down and read the word. That's right, it was:

Wait. No, sorry. That was what the babies were made of. I'll just tell you.

It was **VERY VERY** surprising!

So surprising that Lobbo let out a high-pitched, 'AAGH!'

And it was only after he'd released the scream that his genius brain could work out how it had all happened.

But when it did, it only took 0.00005 seconds for him to cry, 'This is amazing. This is fantabulous. This is an Anti-Stink miracle! **QUICK! CATCH THEM! WE NEED TO LEAVE SOON. I WANT THEM TIED TO MY EXPERIMENTING TABLE READY FOR MY RETURN. WHAT AN UNEXPECTED AFTER-SHOW TREAT!!'**

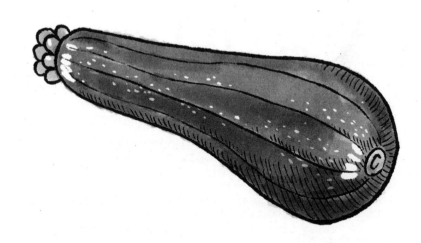

CHAPTER 31

GEE GEED GOO!

But the bogey babies weren't having any of that.

'**GAAAAAAAAAAAAAAAAAAAAAAAAA!**' they cried at the ***LAB RATS***, which meant, 'Keep your nasty mitts off us!'

Then what happened next happened so quickly, I'll have to use slow motion to show you:

IIINNN AAA WWWHHHIIIRRRLLL OFFFFF SSSTTTIIICCCKKKYYY SSSNNNOOOTTT,

OFFFFF TTTHHHEEEYYY LLLEEEAAAPPPTTT IIINNNTTTOOO TTTHHHEEE

AAAIIIRRR LLLIIIKKKEEE GGGOOOOOOEEEYYY RRROOOCCCKKKEEETTTSS

TTTOOOWWWAAARRRDDDSSS . . .

Sorry, slow motion is hard to read. Here. Just imagine this next bit's slow.

In a whirl of sticky snot, off they leapt into the air like gooey rockets towards the lab ceiling, where they rebounded like squidgy, monster-shaped bouncy balls, before splatting on the floor and leaping on the glass wall in front of the courgette garden.

Fear not, stinkers. None of this hurt. The sneeze babies were part clingenglob, so had fantastic sticking power, and part goo-yo (those surprising bogeys that start small, but yo-yo far out of your nostrils), so they could stretch A LOT.

'W-what are you waiting for?' cried Lobbo, watching his troupe run all over the place like headless ... well, lab rats. 'Catch them!'

But the **L∂B R∂TS** were already doing all they could: Bendy was balancing on the Anti-Stink laser, trying to scrape one baby off the window with a long pole. Daphne was standing on Bogey's cage, trying to catch another as it flew past, and every time Lil Hunk (the fastest of the lot thanks to his copter reflexes) caught any of them, it

slipped straight through his fingers like slime.

And for a moment, it looked like the bogeys were winning. That they were causing enough of a hullabagoo (or should that be a hullabaloo? No, 'hullabagoo' will goo, I mean do) to hold off the attack and – if Bogey could work out how to open the cage – even, eventually, all escape.

But alas, there was a problem.

'**STAY WHERE YOU ARE OR YOUR FATHER GETS IT!**' cried Lobbo, suddenly pointing the Anti-Stink laser at Bogey. 'I've zapped him once! Maybe this time he'll explode.'

The babies, now all on the glass wall, stopped dead in their tracks and slid down towards Lil Hunk, Bendy and Daphne, leaving smears of snot in their wake.

'That's better,' said Lobbo as the babies landed in the Lab Rats' hands.

'**GOOOOOOOOO!**' cried Bogey, which meant, '**NOOOOOOOOO! THIS CAN'T BE HAPPENING!**'

But it was happening, all right! And Bogey – stuck behind bars and as exhausted as a snozzflop (you know,

those lightweight boogers that plop out your hooter and float to the ground) – couldn't do a thing about it!

Frank, Tiffany, he thought, closing his eyes and trying to visualize where they might be, **GEE GEED GOO** (which meant, *We need you*). But as he thought it, he felt sad and hopeless. Because after his terrifying behaviour, he knew his friends would never come looking for him. He'd just have to face facts: he and his babies were on their own!

CHAPTER 32

LONG DARK TUNNEL!

'**I**'ve got a bad feeling, Tiffany. My nose is tingling more than ever,' said Frank, as they ended their second sneak around the outside of the concrete bunker. 'We need to get inside RIGHT NOW! But how?' He'd rarely felt such urgency and yet here they were, maybe just metres from Bogey beyond the wall, and they'd not found a single door or window to get through.

'Let's go back to those vehicle tracks,' suggested Tiffany. They'd found a spot where thick wheel marks went right up to the wall. 'Maybe we missed an opening or a button or something.'

Frank followed, but after yet more unsuccessful searching, he slumped to the ground with his back against the wall. 'Oh, this is impossible!' He thought he'd explode. 'We'll never get inside.'

'Let's not panic just yet,' said Tiffany, trying to hide her own panic. 'Let's talk things through while Binky circles round to keep an eye out. And the slugs need a stretch.' She undid the jar lid. 'They've been inside for too long.'

Tiffany poured Sammy, Violet, Peach and Slim on to the grass, where they ooched straight over to a nearby football-sized rock. 'Right. Let's think,' she said to Frank. 'If there are no doors or windows, how could the *LAB RATS* get in?'

Frank shrugged. 'The helipad?'

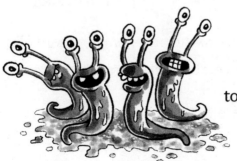

'Yeah, but they can't travel by helicopter all the time. And the roof's too high to climb up to from the ground.'

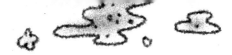

'Maybe they climb a tree?'

'Doubt it. Look – there aren't any branches that get close enough.'

'Ladder, then?'

'Maybe! Yes. Perhaps that's what we should be looking for?'

Suddenly, Peach did a backflip and landed tail-up on Tiffany's hand.

'Well done.' She tickled Peach's belly. 'But we're out the competition, remember? We don't need to practise.' But Peach didn't backflip herself back or ooze away as if she'd made a mistake. She jiggled her tail in the direction of the other slugs.

'Erm, Tiffany,' said Frank, suddenly feeling a sizzle of hope. 'I don't think Peach was practising. I think she was trying to tell us something.'

The friends rushed over to the other slugs, where Slim was spinning clockwise on his back like a mini breakdancer on the rock.

Binky flapped down to watch.

'What's he doing?' said Frank.

'Dunno,' said Tiffany. 'I didn't teach him that move.' Then she gasped. 'Frank, I think he's telling us to –' she felt a bit silly saying this next bit – 'turn the rock?'

'Well, anything's worth a try,' said Frank, grabbing it and trying to twist it clockwise. But it wouldn't budge.

He tried again, pushing with all his might this time, but it still wouldn't budge.

'Let me help,' said Tiffany, **'HRMMMMMMM!'**

They heave-hoed hard. Frank could feel his arm muscles start to burn, and was about to say, 'Let's go back to our ladder plan', when – **'WHOA!'** – the rock moved and the ground began to shake!

And a quiet hissing sound filled the air.

And slowly, smoothly, the concrete wall they'd been leaning on parted to reveal . . . a long dark tunnel!

'WOW!' Frank gasped. 'Binky, you keep watch out here. **We're in!'**

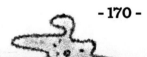

CHAPTER 33

POP! POP! POP!

To say the tunnel was scary would be an understatement. They couldn't use Tiffany's phone torch or someone might see them, so they had to inch along the tunnel walls in the pitch-black, their hearts a-pounding and their ears and eyes (and eye tentacles) a-straining for any kind of movement.

Then, suddenly, the wall disappeared and a small automatic light came on, and the friends saw:

'**GOOLIEMALOOLIE!**' Frank cried in a heavy whisper – something I call a 'whisp-cry' – 'It's **THE LAB RATS**'

MOTORBIKES!'

And then:

POP! POP! POP! POP! POP! POP!

POP!

POP!

Did you hear that, stinkers?

'Twasn't the sound of a snot slop. Or Frank's bum burplets. (Since **THE STINK** had subsided, I'm pleased to say *that* episode is behind us all. Probably. Actually, I don't know.) Nor was it the sound of Slim unsticking himself from Peach's left eye tentacle (though he had accidentally stood on it). No. 'Twas the sound of thoughts coming together in Frank's and Tiffany's heads as it dawned on them who was behind their misfortune.

'**THE LAB RATS**!' they whisp-cried together.

'Of course! Lobbo must be a real scientist!' said Tiffany. 'Their name . . . their sciencey songs . . . Why didn't we think of it before?'

POP!

'And look!' she continued, staring at the name, written

in glitter on a shiny silver bike. 'If you rearrange **LOBBO**, what do you get?'

'**Oblob**,' Frank offered.

'No. Well, yes. But no.' Frank had never been good at anagrams.

'**B-O-B-L-O**,' Tiffany spelt out.

'So he must have made those Boblo pellets to create **THE STINK**.'

POP!

Frank gave the tyre of the silver bike a quick kick. 'Come to think of it, the Snotland Yard policeman was wearing a hoop earring, just like Lobbo.'

'And that beefy guy in the group has helicopter tattoos!' said Tiffany.

'And the two women, well, they've always looked nasty!' said Frank.

POP! POP! POP!

Of course, you knew all this already stinkers, but Frank and Tiffany didn't and the realization made their heads whirl and their teeth chatter and their ears wiggle and

their big toes flip up in their shoes, which was well weird.

Then Frank felt himself fill with anger.

How dare the singers do this to them! How dare they endanger Bogey! Dear, kind, clever and miraculous Bogey. He wanted to kick and scream. But he was so worried, he pushed it out of his mind. 'Come on,' he whisp-cried again.

But they couldn't, could they, because there was . . .

'A voice-activated door. Oh no!'

The friends stared at each other in disbelief. They'd come so far. And for what? To get thwarted by a doorway.

'I can't believe it!' said Tiffany.

'I bet it's that rotter Lobbo's voice we need. We'll never get through!' said Frank, feeling his innards swirl and whirl in dismay.

Tiffany looked sad. Then gasped. 'Wait!' She rifled through her pocket to draw out her phone. 'Frank, I recorded Lobbo singing on my phone at the semi-final, remember? I bet it's still on here somewhere!'

And, stinkers, it was!

And so, after an annoyingly long search through her

phone, 'cause it's always when you need to go fast on phones that you can't . . .

'*AHHHHHHHHHHHHHHHHHHHH!*'

Out came Lobbo's spectacular top B from Tiffany's phone.

And HISSSSSS went the door.

It was time to find Bogey!

CHAPTER 34

SOMETHING TERRIBLE!

Now, stinkers, it's not that Frank and Tiffany's walk through Lobbo's high-tech bunker was boring. It most certainly was not. It was p-pee-in-y-your-p-pants terrifying - which is exciting if you ask me, 'cause I'm not the one doing it! It's just that things are getting increasingly worse for the bogeys as I write, so I need to whizz us there fast, without touring the bunker.

Here's how.

You shout a silly word and imagine Frank and Tiffany slinking cautiously down the corridors (led by the tickling in Frank's nose, and wondering, how – once they'd found Big Bogey – they'd turn him back to his normal size then get them all home) and I'll move us quickly through the rooms.

OK? Ready?

Good.

Shout . . .

FLOBBER!

We've flitted through the Science Station.

PLOOP!

We've zipped across the soundproofed Tune Room.

WINKLE!

We've sped over the dressing rooms.

HINKY-DINK!

We've made a quick stop at the computerized toilets with self-heating seats! (Sorry, but when you gotta go . . . !)

IPPLE!

And now we're in the high-tech greenhouse, where five-metre-long courgettes are hanging off ginormous stems above Boblo's green fertilizer slime. And Frank, Tiffany

and the slugs are quaking in their boots (and foot fringes) at the scene beyond the glass wall.

What was the scene?

Oh, something terrible, stinkers:

'Bogey's back to normal,' whisp-cried Frank. (Sorry, that wasn't the terrible bit. It's this bit now.) 'But he's in a cage and . . . and . . .' Frank couldn't get his words out, it was so horrible to see.

There, looking meaner than ever, were Daphne, Lil Hunk and Bendy, trying to strap what looked like bogey babies on to the science table, with Lobbo (already dressed in his flashy lab coat for the show) pointing a big laser machine at them, and Bogey - exhausted and helpless - just watching on in horror!

'WILL. YOU. JUST. GET. IN!' grunted Daphne, squishing one baby under the first strap. 'We've gotta go in a minute!'

The baby had been struggling, but - SQUELCH! - it went in, with its little flat head bulging out over the top of the strap.

'AND YOU!' cried Lil Hunk.

'AND YOU!' squeaked Bendy.

Frank felt his heart do a triple backflip and flop on his belly. 'Tiffany, are you seeing this?'

'Y-Yes! B-Bogey b-babies, Frank! How—?'

'I don't know,' he said, his heart beating a million-gazillion miles an hour. 'But they must have come from Bogey, which means they're his family, which means they're our family now, which means –' **GOOLIEMALOOLIE!** *What sort*

of crazed rotters were they up against? – 'we need to save them first and ask how it happened later.' He ripped off a big baby courgette and brandished it like a stick.

'What's that for?' whispered Tiffany.

'To defend Bogey.'

'OK.' She ripped one off too.

Then, without thinking of their own safety, Frank and Tiffany jumped up and dashed through the door.

CHAPTER 35

VANISHED!

'**S**TAY AWAY FROM THEM!**'** Frank shouted, swinging the courgette. They really should have come better prepared.

Bogey immediately let out a whopper of a **'GOOOOOOOOOOOOOOOOOOOOO!'**, which meant: 'Frank, Tiffany, you came for me. I'm SOOOO SORRY. For everything! And look – I'm a dad!'

To which Frank replied with a look that Bogey knew meant: *There's nothing to be sorry for, Bogey. None of this was your fault and **WE LOVE YOU – AND YOUR***

CHILDREN!

'Twas a beautiful moment.

But it didn't last long.

'GET OFF!' cried Frank and Tiffany, as Lil Hunk grabbed them with just one muscly arm, snapping their courgettes before tying their hands and legs to the experiment table below the bogey babies, the Anti-Stink laser now pointing at them all. The slugs, between Tiffany's feet in their jar, tried to fight their way out, but Tiffany had screwed the lid on too tightly.

Lobbo twisted his quiff, did a little boogie and sang *'Welcoooome!'* in his signature top B, as if he were on stage. 'I thought you might hunt for your friend. But I didn't think you'd ever get in. I'm *almost* impressed!'

Frank pulled at the straps so hard the table shook, but he still couldn't free his hands.

'Now, don't get me wrong – I don't need you. You're already disqualified.' Lobbo wicksmirked. 'But now you are here, I'll keep you 'til the competition's over . . . or until the world tour's finished . . . or maybe longer! I could

do with some new rats to experiment on. HA!' He did a little twirl. 'How fun is this, Lab Rats? I'd secretly hoped at least one other Snozzler'd come, 'cause, well, I've been wanting to gloat! And now there are two ... A one, a two ... A one, two, three, four ...'

His troupe immediately burst into a little song and dance:

'Shame, shame, shame,
The world won't know your name.
You used to be our rivals
Now it's us who've won the finals!
Yeah!
Shame, shame, shame,
Now the world won't kno-oow
Yo-ur naaaaaaaaame!'

'Ta-da!' cried Lobbo with a little hand shimmy at the end. Daphne, Bendy and Lil Hunk took a bow.

Frank, Tiffany and Bogey (still overwhelmed that his friends were *really* there) couldn't believe their eyes and ears. The rockers were off their . . . erm . . . rockers!

'This is why you've done this?' Frank screamed. 'For a competition?' His eyes flitted between Bogey and the babies. How he wished he could free them. Let them know they were safe. They all looked terrified and Bogey looked extra panicked for his family.

'Not just any competition,' replied Lobbo. 'The one that'll make me . . . ehem . . . US . . . famous beyond our wildest dreams. And, well, I love a show, so I couldn't get you disqualified without some THEATRE, could I?'

'But you made Bogey go viral. You caused all that damage to Honkerty. You've ruined everything for us. And you can't just keep us here,' cried Tiffany.

'Who's gonna stop me?' said Lobbo. 'Teehee!'

Frank couldn't believe he was hearing this. 'B-but fame's not the most important thing in life,' he blurted. 'You can be famous one day and forgotten the next. It's friends and family that count.' He thought about the Snozzlers and

how much he loved them and wanted to see them again –
much more than winning any competition. 'And, anyway,
who wins by sabotaging their rivals?' he continued. 'The
best winners win by being the best.'

(I know, stinkers. Frank was very wise for a young boy,
that's why I write about him.)

'WOOOO! Listen to you, Mr Morals,' Lobbo mocked.
The **LAB RATS** snickered.

But there was no time for anything else, because
suddenly, unexpectedly (gosh, stinkers, grab a Bikkie-
Wikkie!) the babies started growling tiny 'GRRRS' and in
a blink of an eye dissolved into snot puddles. Not snot
puddles like the ones Bogey had left behind when he'd
grown, but thick, moving snot puddles – rather like the
sneeze globs they'd started out as, except with faces. And
within seconds they'd slopped out from under their straps,
and re-formed to ERUPT into the air like pent-up green
lava.

And then everything blurred into one.
ONE!

See it?

No?

OK, I'll break it down:

Number 1) Flying through the air in a V-shaped formation, the babies whooshed straight towards the door

to the high-tech greenhouse to escape, but Lil Hunk got there first and slammed it closed, causing them to boing straight off the glass and (stinkers, I can't bear to

look!) fly towards the red **EMERGENCY SELF-DESTRUCT button** on the wall.

'NOOOOOOO!' screamed Lobbo, dashing to stop them.

But he was too late, and – **SPLAT! SPLAT! SPLAT!** – they hit it, one after the other, before bouncing back to the top of Bogey's cage.

'COUNTDOWN TO SELF-DESTRUCTION BEGIIIIIINS!' came Lobbo's expert rock-singing voice over the speakers in the wall.

'YOU'VE GOT TWO MINUTES 'TIL IT BLOOOOOOOWS!'

'GE-GE-GE!' Lobbo froze for a moment in his glittery boots and couldn't get his words out.

But that wasn't the worst of it.

The worst of it was **Number 2)**

As he dashed towards his lab computer to override the countdown (he'd set a safety timer, giving him five seconds to reverse the explosion), he slipped on some goo and whooshed into the Anti-Stink laser he'd been pointing at his prisoners, bumped the switch, and –

CRZZZZZZZZZZZZZZZZ

– fired a beam!

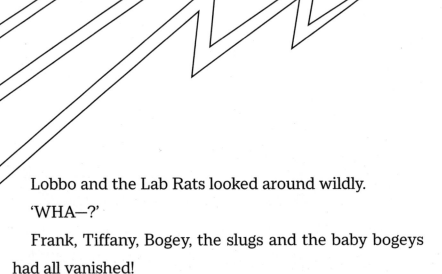

Lobbo and the Lab Rats looked around wildly.

'WHA—?'

Frank, Tiffany, Bogey, the slugs and the baby bogeys
had all vanished!

CHAPTER 36

'HELP!'

Don't worry, stinkers. When I said 'vanished', it's because I didn't know then what I'm about to tell you now, which is . . .

They weren't *totally* gone!

Phew!

But you will need a magnifying glass to see them.

Oh!

I know.

You see, the Anti-Stink laser hadn't filled them with gas (as Lobbo had suggested it might), it had shrunk-stunk

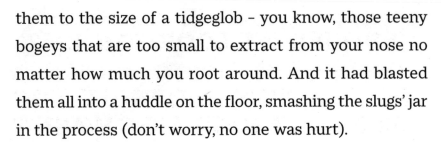

them to the size of a tidgeglob – you know, those teeny bogeys that are too small to extract from your nose no matter how much you root around. And it had blasted them all into a huddle on the floor, smashing the slugs' jar in the process (don't worry, no one was hurt).

'HELP!' Frank and Tiffany cried.

'GOO!' shouted Bogey and the babies.

'MEEP!' went the slugs, who were practically microscopic.

But it was a total waste of energy, 'cause they were so tiny, no one could hear them.

Frank looked around. The straps that had bound them were now mountainous coils, the shards of the broken slug jar had become jagged icebergs, Bogey's cage seemed taller than a skyscraper, and the lab looked like an endless, gigantic city. Just getting to the door might take a week – and they didn't have that long. What were they going to do?

'ER, LOBBO,' said Lil Hunk suddenly.

'ARGH!' The Minis (as I'll now call 'em) thought their heads would burst. To their now-tiny ears, his voice boomed like

a jet engine.

'SHOULD WE LOOK FOR 'EM?'

Lobbo stared at the spot where the kids and bogeys had once stood. **'IT'S PROBABLY TOO LATE,'** he said. **'THAT LASER WASN'T DESIGNED FOR FIRING ON TO NORMAL-SIZED THINGS.'**

'But, we're here!' Frank and Tiffany screamed, despite reeling from the ear pain. The Lab Rats were lots of bad things – crooks, Bogeynappers, prisoner-keepers, cheats, total egomaniacs – but in that second, they were also their only hope.

Alas, stinkers, it wasn't to be.

'AND ANYWAY, WE'RE BETTER OFF WITHOUT THEM,' Lobbo continued. **'THEY CAN'T TELL TALES IF THEY'VE POPPED IT.'**

Frank couldn't believe it.

'QUICK. I MISSED THE SAFETY TIMER. THE WHOLE BUNKER'S

GONNA BLOW! IF WE DON'T WANT TO DIE, WE NEED TO GET OUT, NOW. TO THE FINAL!' He ran towards the door.

'BUT—'

'OH, DON'T BLUB, DAPHNE. YOU BUILT IT ONCE, YOU CAN BUILD ANOTHER ONE.'

And just like that, the Lab Rats all scarpered off to the competition final!

'ONE MINUTE 'TIL IT BLOOOOOOOWS!'

Lobbo's recording came in again over the speakers.

Frank and Tiffany covered their ears. Then they panicked.

'WHAT ARE WE GOING TO DO?' cried Frank (Sorry, tiny squeaky voices are hard to read, aren't they. I hope you grabbed that magnifying glass earlier. You're gonna need it.) 'No one else knows we're here, so no one will look for us.'

'I DON'T KNOW! I DON'T KNOW. I CAN'T THINK OF ANYTHING!' cried Tiffany, hugging her slugs tight.

Frank put his arm around Bogey and the babies.

'THIRTY SECONDS 'TIL IT BLOOOOOOOOOOOOOWS,' Lobbo's recording came in again.

'GOOLIEMALOOLIE! WE'RE GONNA DIE!' Frank squealed.

And as soon as he'd squealed it, the ground started to vibrate. Just a quiver for you, but a proper, full-on mega earthquake for the friends and babies, and they were tossed around the floor like ragdolls.

'TWENTY SECONDS 'TIL IT BLOOOOOOOOOOOOOWS.'

This is it, thought Frank, a tiddler rolling down his cheek (it's what you call a tear when you've been shrunk). He wobbled on one leg. *I'll never see Mum or Dad again. And there's nothing I can do.*

He struggled over to Tiffany, who was sobbing, and then to Bogey and the baby bogeys. Then they hugged for comfort.

And that's when something amazing happened.

CHAPTER 37

BOOM!

In a flurry of dust and flapping, a small brown bat fluttered in through an air vent.

'BINKY!' Frank and Tiffany cried.

And I say small, but to the Minis, Binky was the size of a bus and her flapping was as loud as Lil Hunk's chopper.

'Soaring slugs!' said Tiffany.

'Bogey, did you call her?' asked Frank.

Bogey nodded. He'd sensed she was there!

'WOW!' Having a friend who could talk to bats with his mind was AMAZING!

Binky landed next to them with the force of a hurricane (or it felt that way).

'TEN SECONDS 'TIL IT BLOOOOOOOOOOOOOWS.'

'Quick!' cried Frank. 'On to her back.'

The friends scrambled on as fast as they could, giving each other a leg-up (or a backflip-up), and catching each other's hands (or eye tentacles) when they slipped, 'cause Binky had very silky fur.

(If you want to know the seating order, it went Frank, the babies, Bogey and Tiffany, then the slugs at the back.)

'FIVE SECONDS 'TIL IT BLOOOOOOOOOOOOOWS! AND THE COUNT DOWN BEGINS. FIVE . . .'

'QUICK! WE NEED TO GO, NOOOOOOW!' screamed Frank.

'FOUR . . .'

Binky immediately took off like a bullet towards the air vent.

'THREE . . .'

She swooped inside the vent, but it was long and dark and they couldn't see where it ended. Frank and Tiffany screamed as the building started to rumble like thunder around them.

'TWO . . .'

The screws holding the metal walls of the vent together suddenly started to pop out like deadly missiles. It was as if the bunker was folding in on itself.

PEW!

PEW!

PEW!

Binky had to twist and turn to avoid them.

'ONE . . .'

A HUGE EXPLOSION FILLED THE AIR!

BOOM!

Dust and spiky slithers of metal entered the vent behind Binky and careered towards them all like a deadly wall.

'FASTER!' screamed Frank. The death-dust was closing in. The air felt thick and hot, and sharp pointy things whizzed past them, missing them by micrometres. No one had ever felt so scared.

'GOOOO! GOOOOO!' cried Bogey (which meant 'HELP! HELP!')

But it was no good, because they were hurtling towards a **DEAD END**.

And

THERE WAS NO WAY OUT!

CHAPTER 38

SPLAT!

Binky and the Minis smashed into the metal!

SPLAT!

The End

STOP!

Sorry, stinkers. That's simply not true.

I don't know why I wrote that.

Get that image out of your head.

THE MINIS DID NOT HIT THE DEAD END.

I repeat:

THE MINIS DID NOT HIT THE DEAD END.

They didn't hit it because there wasn't one.

It was a sharp bend that just looked like a dead end.

And in one second flat, with a nifty side spin, Binky had turned it and whooshed them all outside, one nanosecond before the bunker caved into the ground in a **DEAFENING RUMBLE**, leaving nothing but rubble and smoke pouring into the clearing of ~~FLUFFY FAIRY WOOD~~ **PRIVATE PROPERTY – KEEP OUT OR DIE WOOD**.

CHAPTER 39

GAAAARMA GONK

Are you all right, stinkers?

Did you have to eat an entire batch of Bikkie-Wikkies?

I did. Right when the friends got shrunk. And right at that corner moment at the end. **BRRRR!**

But don't worry, all the stressful parts are over now, 'cause the Minis had started their journey back to Snozzle Castle.

STOP. Sorry. That's not quite right.

Why?

Because arriving at the castle tidgeglob-size would be very dangerous. They could get accidentally squished by Mum and Dad, or wiped away, or sucked up by a vacuum, or worse!

'We could get accidentally squished by Mum and Dad,' said Frank as the castle's turrets appeared in the distance. 'Or wiped away, or sucked up by a vacuum, or worse!' (See, told you!) It was already all they could do to hold on to Binky in the wind. Frank didn't dare think how helpless they'd be in such a huge house. 'We need to think of a way to get back to size before we go back.'

He sounded calm on the outside, but inside he was mushier than a slop-pat (which is a very squishy bogey). What if they never got back to their normal size? What if they had to stay like this for ever? And eat crumbs? And live in tiny cracks? And never speak to their families again. *NOOOOOOOOOOOOOOOOOO!* screamed his brain.

It was time to think.

Everyone thunk . . . thinked . . . erm, started thinking – including Binky.

Then Frank stopped thinking, 'cause he couldn't keep his eyes off the babies – they were so much like Bogey. Yet different. And he loved them already. He just hoped they'd all get out of this alive, so they could get to know one another.

And then he started thinking again, 'cause, well, this was a terrible situation and he wasn't going to solve it by gazing at his new family.

'Maybe the police could help us?' said Tiffany, as they flew over traffic jams. It looked like even more people had watched the viral videos of Bogey and were trying to get into the village to see what was going on. She was sure one of the vehicles down there was a police car. 'We could try and find a way to call them.'

'But we're too small. Even if we found a way to call, they'd never hear us talk,' said Frank. 'Oh, if only we could bring back **THE STINK** that grew Bogey,' he said. 'Maybe that'd make us grow?'

Bogey suddenly sat bolt upright, and gathered the babies to him. 'GAAAAAA!' he said.

'Yeah, but I bet all Lobbo's extra Boblo pellets disappeared with the bunker,' said Tiffany.

Bogey shook his head. 'GAAAARMA GONK!'

Frank gasped. 'He's right! Farmer Plonk's field. There are bound to be some stray pellets there.'

And so, with a flap of Binky's wings and a GASP from everyone as they swooped over the village and got a proper bird's-eye view of the growing crowds around the castle (we're talking tens of thousands here), the Minis landed, carefully, at the foot of one of Farmer Plonk's whopper

corn plants, and Binky fluttered off for a well-deserved rest.

VERY IMPORTANT NOTICE

Now, stinkers, the following instructions are for what you should do if you ever find yourself shrunk by the Anti-Stink, like the Minis.

It's what Frank, Tiffany, the slugs and the bogeys did. Though I can't promise it worked for them (we haven't got that far in the story yet), but when

you're tidgeglob-size and the rest of your life is in play, anything's worth a try, so I'd read on very carefully.

STEP 1: Locate a stray Boblo pellet.

The Minis did just that, right on the edge of a mountain ridge (which was really a little furrow in the still-green soil).

STEP 2: Get the pellet wet.

That was easy. There was a puddle right by the pellet. They rolled it into the water and . . .

'Oh, it's fizzing!' said Frank. Then 'URGH!' as the horrid whiff of Stink hit their nostrils.

STEP 3: Wait.

Not for long.

Instantly, the bogeys felt grumpy and everyone began to bottom-burp.

But then, seconds later, all the Minis felt a tingling rush through their bodies. And their feet started to shake. And their muscles started to bulge. And their legs shot up (or foot fringes shot down, for the slugs). Then their arms (and eye tentacles) elongated. Followed by their necks.

And finally, to everyone's relief, their grumpiness and trumpeteering disappeared and their heads ballooned back to their previous size.

'**GOOLIEMALOOLIE!** We're back!' shouted Frank.

'Cause they were.

And once they'd all checked every human finger, bogey toe and slug foot was still in place, they hugged and rushed back to the castle.

CHAPTER 40

B-BOGEY!

'**AHHHHHHHHHHHHHHHHHHHHHHHH!**' cried Mum in a G so high the windows rattled.

But she wasn't singing.

No.

She was wailing from **SHOCK** and **RELIEF** and **JOY** as Frank and Tiffany (slugs and Binky in tow) stepped through the secret door into Frank's bedroom.

But that was nothing compared to the commotion that followed as Tiffany's parents whisked her and the slugs into a hug. And Dad (accidentally standing on Mum's toe) practically jumped on Frank. And words like –

'HOW DARE YOU SNEAK OUT!'

'WE LOVE YOU!'

'WHERE ON EARTH HAVE YOU BEEN?'

'WAIT! IS THAT A SECRET DOOR IN THE WALL?'

'WE THOUGHT YOU'D BEEN KIDNAPPED!'

'DON'T EVER RUN OFF AGAIN!'

– filled the air, right before an astonished:

'B-BOGEY?' as Bogey stepped out of the tunnel looking sheepish.

And then more words came out, like –

'Oh my g-goodness is that really you?'

'How did you get back to size?'

'OH! OH! OH!'

– followed by:

'AHHHHHHHHHHHHHHHHHHHHH!' as the bogey

babies came out from behind him and clung to his legs!

At which point, Frank thought he'd better tell his and Tiffany's families everything. And if they were going to stop Lobbo from ever using his Stink to harm anyone again, he had to make them believe him.

'Mums and dads,' he started in his most serious voice. 'Please meet the WHOLE Bogey family.'

'WH—?' said Dad.

GLUPS! went Tiffany's parents.

Mum's jaw dropped. 'H-how did—' She looked woozy.

'Bogey said he got shrunk back to size by Lobbo's laser, which made him sneeze. Then he cried and his tears made the snot globs come to life.' Frank patted the babies' heads. 'We think **THE STINK** made it happen.' (Sorry, stinkers, if you're wondering when Bogey had told this to Frank, it was somewhere off-page between chapters thirty-eight and thirty-nine,

while flying on Binky.)

'Lobbo? Laser?' said Mum, incredibly confused.

'Oh, yeah, sorry,' Frank said, realizing he'd gone too far too fast. So he started again, at the beginning. And then there was no stopping him as he told them about:

* **the snot trail they'd followed to Lobbo's bunker**
* **the Snotland Yard helicopter on the roof**
* **the fertilizer pellets in Lobbo's courgette room – the same ones that had made THE STINK in Plonk's field**
* **Bogey (back to normal size) with the babies, imprisoned**
* **the Lab Rats tying them all up**

Hang on, why am I telling *you* this? You already know what happened. Here, I'll fast-forward to the last thing that Frank said, which was . . .

'And so, once the self-destruct button had been hit, and we'd been shrunk to the size of a tidgeglob, the Lab Rats scarpered. We'd all be dead if Bogey hadn't summoned Binky from the woods to fly us out the air vent and back to Farmer Plonk's field where we found a stray fertilizer pellet.'

Frank was met with stunned silence.

Then Dad clapped – 'What a fantastic film plot, son' – until Mum elbowed him.

'If it's just a film plot, how come Bogey's back to normal and he's a dad?' said Frank.

'Erm . . .' No one could answer that.

Then silence filled the air AGAIN as it dawned on all the grown-ups that everything their children had said was true.

'We're so sorry!' cried Mum and Dad, rushing over to hug Bogey.

'We've been terrible. We should have helped you,' Mum sobbed. Frank had never seen her look so guilty. 'You saved their lives! We love you. We've always loved you . . . it's just . . .'

'GOOOO!' said Bogey, which meant, 'It's all right. I know I was pretty terrifying.' Then the babies suddenly boinged on to Mum's lap and gave her a sloppy kiss, so she cuddled them and felt a bit better.

'You *were* terrifying,' said Dad, suddenly looking thoughtful. 'Which - thinking back, is . . . BRILLIANT!' He hugged Bogey too. 'I could use that sort of scariness in my next film . . . if you'll forgive us and agree to star in it . . . and the babies and Binky of course.' He turned to the bat.

'**GOOOO!**', '**GAAA!**' and **FLAP!** went all the bogeys and Binky together, which meant, 'WE'D LOVE TO!'

'What are we waiting for?' Frank suddenly cried. They couldn't hang round all day explaining and making up. 'We've got some Lab Rats to stop!'

And so, as Honkerty's weird hedgehog (who, I'm pleased to say, had survived the flooding) impersonated a police officer again somewhere over in the village, off they all went – pushing through the ever-growing crowds outside – to drive to the ***FORGET THE REST, YOU'RE THE BEST*** final and tell the world the truth about the Lab Rats.

CHAPTER 41

TRUEY-WOOEY-TRUE-TRUE

O ver in the Blob-Warble Theatre in the city of Warble-Blob, not half an hour later, the crowds at the **FORGET THE REST, YOU'RE THE BEST** final were going wild.

'LAB RATS, LAB RATS, LAB RATS!' they chanted as Lobbo got to the end of the band's signature song, 'I've Got My Ion You'.

'I love science.
So do you.

Our atoms attract like chemical glue.
Whoa, oh oh baby,
I've got my ion – I. O. N. – on you!'

'**BRAVO, BRAVO!'** Judge Dicky Dingaling stepped past the TV cameras and on to the stage with a golden heart-shaped trophy.

The **L∂B R∂TS** took a bow and made extra little smoke-people come out of their bike exhausts to much applause, then they looked up to see the room alight with a myriad of square blue screens as people filmed the scene with their phones.

'**Ahhhh, they LOVE US!'** Lobbo shouted to the Rats.

'**WAHOOOO!'** the Rats replied. Bendy did the splits.

Then Lobbo strutted across the stage in his sparkly platform shoes, egging on the crowd

for more applause. He'd never felt so powerful. He was about to get the trophy of his **D.R.E.A.M.S.** Who cares if he'd made the kids and snotsters disappear. It hadn't been his intention. And now the bunker had exploded, no one would ever find out. *Ha.* Now nothing stood between the **LAB RATS** and their fame. Erm, who was he kidding? Between HIM and HIS FAME. Just the thought of it made his bum dance and his heart sing.

'Now, as you know, it's been an unusual year for the competition,' Judge Dingaling began, speaking into the TV camera. 'With some *monumental* last-minute disqualifications resulting in only one band qualifying for the final today.'

The audience chuckled. Everyone had seen the 'giant Bogey' videos.

'And so . . .'

Wait for it. Wait for it. Lobbo could feel it coming.

'. . . it is an immense pleasure to present this year's ***FORGET THE REST, YOU'RE THE BEST*** trophy to . . .'

The crowd hushed. A drum roll resounded around the

theatre.

Lobbo took a deep breath . . .

'To the only troupe left in the competition. The wonderful, the glittery, the one-of-a-kind . . . *LAB RA—*'

'STOP!'

came a loud voice through a megaphone as hundreds of police officers stormed the theatre.

What?

How?

Remember Honkerty's weird hedgehog? Well, it turns out that when he'd impersonated a police officer, he'd explained everything that had happened to the Snozzlers (Binky'd told him most of it after her rest), and his voice had somehow been picked up on a police radio, where it had tipped off an officer

called Phil.

Name ring a bell?

It should.

PC Phil was none other than the man who'd arrested Lobbo for his Stink the first time round, and now he'd heard the story and seen Bogey's viral videos, he had all the proof he needed for another arrest.

The audience and Dicky Dingaling gasped as the police surrounded the Lab Rats.

TV cameras immediately swung round to film the action.

'WHA—?' Lobbo squealed a loud top C in horror. **'NO! Not PC Phil! This can't be true! NOT AGAIN!'**

But alas (for him), it was very true – something I call **truey-wooey-true-true**.

And before anyone could say **STINKUS-DINKUS-INUS-NOZZLEUS-HORRIBLIS**, Lobbo, Lil Hunk, Bendy and Daphne were all in cuffs and PC Phil had grabbed Judge Dingaling's mic to explain everything to the entertainment-hungry crowds, who either gleefully filmed

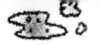

every last second of it on their phones or watched it on TV at home.

Oh, Lobbo had become super-mega famous all right. But not in the way he'd hoped. In the nasty way. In the sort of way where everyone knows your name 'cause you're a proper rotten crook!

CHAPTER 42

'BOGEY! BOGEY! BOGEY!'

'**S**TOP!' yelled Frank, as his friends and family piled into the already packed theatre, trailed by hordes of people who had followed them from outside the castle.

He made a beeline for the TV cameras and prepared himself to explain, but Tiffany grabbed his arm. 'Look!'

'**GOOLIEMALOOLIE!**' he cried, as he realized the police were already there and had arrested the *LAB RATS*! They'd arrived too late! 'How—?'

'Beats me,' said Tiffany, as a huge spotlight swung round

to illuminate the Snozzlers.

'How did you lot surv—?' Lobbo started to shout, fuming, but he stopped himself. He'd wanted to say, *How did you lot survive and get back to your normal sizes?* ('Cause, frankly, that was a question worthy of a new science experiment!) But with his hands cuffed, the police there, and the TV cameras and entire audience filming the scene, he decided it was best not to admit he'd done anything wrong. Instead, he belted out his signature top B as the police carted him and the Lab Rats off, and the last thing Frank, Tiffany and Bogey saw of them were flashes of Bendy's long nails, Lil Hunk's copter tattoos, Daphne's frowning face and Lobbo's blond quiff, disappearing through the emergency exit.

'What now?' Tiffany whispered to Frank, suddenly aware that EVERYBODY was filming them. Bogey and the babies were trembling like jelly.

'Erm, I think we should leave too,' whispered Frank, looking at Bogey. 'We were disqualified and no one likes us, remember?' He thought back to the horrible comments on the internet. 'Plus, the babies look scared.'

But as they all started to push past people to get back through the door . . .

PING!

Did you hear that, stinkers?

PING! PING! PING! PING! PING PING PING PING PING PING PING PING PING PING PING PING PING PING PING PING PING PING PING PING PING PING PING PING PING PING PING PING PING PING PING PING PING PING PING PING PING PING PING PING PING PING PING PING PING PING PING PING PING PING PING PING PING PING PING PING PING PING PING PING PING PING PING PING PING PING PING PING PING!

'Twas the sound of more video notifications coming in on everyone's phones inside the theatre.

'SOARING SLUGS! LOOK!' cried Tiffany. There on her screen was video after video of PC Phil explaining what had happened as the Lab Rats got ARRESTED. 'There must be at least ten million views already!'

Then, little by little, the people in the back row started chanting:

'BOGEY!

BOGEY!

BOGEY!'

And it got louder and louder as the other rows joined in.

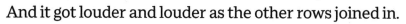

'BOGEY!
BOGEY!
BOGEY!'

And soon, Dicky Dingaling was shouting it too, over his microphone, waving his hand to invite the Snozzlers on to the stage.

'BOGEY!
BOGEY!
BOGEY!'

Frank couldn't believe his eyes or ears. Nobody could.

'What do you think we should do?' he squealed.

'Go on stage,' the grown-ups and Tiffany shouted

back. This was clearly good chanting. ('Twas surprising how fast the people had changed their minds, stinkers, but that's the internet for you - remember that, now!) And it was a wonderful sight and sound to Frank, for it meant that - thanks to PC Phil, an honest man - everyone had finally heard the truth.

𝕿𝖍𝖊 𝕰𝖓𝖉

What? GOSH, NOT AGAIN! Sorry. There's still more.

CHAPTER 43

SHAKE YOUR BOGEY

'This is an unexpected turn of events!' said Judge Dingaling, applauding alongside the wild crowds as the family stepped on to the stage. Tiffany's parents stood in the aisle at the front next to Mike and Rita, who gave them a thumbs up.

'It seems I was a little quick to judge you,' Dingaling whispered to Frank and Bogey away from the mic. 'As a *judge*, I should have known better. Sorry about that!'

'**GOO!**' said Bogey, suddenly pulling him into a whopper sticky hug. All was forgiven.

'So, after everything this lot have been through,' Judge Dingaling continued back into the mic, wiping himself down with a chuckle, 'How about we bend the rules a little? We have shows coming up in New York, London, Sydney and Los Angeles and no one to play them, so I say we proclaim ... **THE SNOZZLERS** ... **THIS YEAR'S WINNERS OF *FORGET THE REST, YOU'RE THE BEST*!**'

The audience applause was deafening.

'Wha—?' cried Frank, Tiffany, Mum and Dad. They would be touring after all!

Frank hadn't heard Paris on the list, but it didn't matter. **'WE'VE WON!!!!!!!!!!!!!!'** he yelled.

'GOO-GOO-GOOEY!' cried all the bogeys, as Binky flapped excitedly overhead.

'Take it away!' said Judge Dingaling, handing Bogey the golden heart-shaped trophy. 'Show us what you can do.'

And at that moment, it didn't matter that the Snozzlers had never found the time to think of a show for the final. They were so happy they'd won and would soon be performing and travelling, that they improvised – even the babies, who were (much to everyone's surprise) remarkably good at singing and playing guitar and drums.

And can you guess the title of the song they made up?

It was 'I Ate a Bad Prawn'!

Nah. Just kidding. It was called 'SHAKE YOUR BOGEY'. And it was proper good fun (scan this and you might even be able to hear it!).

And guess what?

While the babies were singing, and the slugs (who had secretly really enjoyed flying on Binky) took it in turns to do acrobatic backflips to land on Binky's back, Bogey did his first ever dance!

Oh, how I wish you'd been there, stinkers. It was hilarious. Every time the words 'Shake Your Bogey' came up, Bogey touched his nose with one hand and wiggled his bum. It was so catchy, even Mum and Dad and Frank and

Tiffany joined in (though Frank actually picked his nose rather than just touching it). And soon the audience and Dingaling were doing it too (the dancing, not the nose-picking).

Go on - you should give it a try (again, I mean the dancing, not the pickin'). Even without the music, it's fun.

And so, stinkers, I think it's time we leave our happy heroes there to their bogey boogieing, for this time it really is the e—

OH NO, NO, SORRY.
IT'S SNOT . . . ERM, I MEAN IT'S STILL
'NOT' THE END.
I HAVE A FEW MORE THINGS I NEED TO
TELL YOU, IN AN EPILOGUE.
WHAT'S THAT?
YOU KNOW, THE STORY AFTER THE STORY
THAT ONLY THE BEST BOOKS HAVE?
TO GET THERE, YOU'LL HAVE TO MOVE US
FORWARDS IN TIME — ABOUT SIX
MONTHS SHOULD DO IT —

BY SHOUTING **'FARTLEK'**.
WHICH HAS NOTHING TO DO WITH THE STINK!
IT'S A TYPE OF SPORTS TRAINING, WHERE
YOU RUN FAST THEN SLOW, WHICH I BET IS
WHAT YOU DO ON YOUR WAY TO SCHOOL.
YOU LITTLE FARTLEKERS, YOU!

EPILOGUE

As the autumn turned to winter and the winter turned to spring, everything had changed for Frank and the Snozzlers.

Rumour had it that Lobbo - now behind bars in Bing Bang High-Security Prison with the other Lab Rats - no longer wanted fame. He'd tasted the bad side of it with those gazillion videos showing his arrest, and was now quite content using his genius mind to put on science-themed shows with his fellow inmates. **LOBBO'S LAB RATS** now had 3,021 new members (though they couldn't all perform at once, of course) – the news of which had pleasantly surprised Frank.

And the Snozzlers were very happy with their three new sticky family members – all girls, it turns out – who Bogey had decided to call Googoo, Agoo and Gagagoo. The babies were cute, bouncy and very squidgy, but above all else, they loved performing, just like their father. Under their stage name of The Snozzlettes, they'd brought the house down at every single one of the Snozzlers' ***FORGET THE REST, YOU'RE THE BEST*** shows, in New York, London, Sydney and Los Angeles, even if the only words they could pronounce were 'GAAAAA!' and 'GOO!'

But that's not all . . .

Remember all those videos of Bogey's mega-metamorphosis?

Well, after Lobbo's highly televised arrest, they'd captured even more attention (some eighty million, two hundred and twenty-seven thousand and one views . . . no, two . . . no, three – gosh, it just keeps rising), so Judge Dingaling, Mike and Rita had decided to give the

Snozzlers their OWN REALITY TV SHOW called *Me and My Bogeys*. It was to be a twelve-part series, following the Snozzlers gooing (sorry, I mean 'going') about their daily lives as the 'world's most unique' show family.

Frank had said yes, 'cause he thought everyone should see how brilliant and special the bogeys really were.

Bogey had agreed 'cause – through his telepathic communications – he wanted to show everyone how important bats and all other animals are. And show off his amazing kids.

And everyone else had agreed because, well, it was too exciting an opportunity to turn down.

And can you guess where the show was going to take place?

Not in Snozzle Castle.

In space?

No.

On a moving train?

Nah.

If I say croissants, baguette and Eiffel Tower, does that

help?

That's right.

PARIS!

And to Frank it was everything he could have hoped for and more.

'CUT!' cried Mike as the Snozzlers posed with a billboard at the top of the tower, the city spreading under their feet like the most beautiful toy town Frank had ever seen (he understood why Mum and Dad had loved it so much). The slugs backflipped on to Tiffany's shoulder and Binky landed on his. The billboard read –

ME AND MY BOGEYS

The new musical reality show set in Paris
Streaming on Dingaling TV

– and it made Frank's heart boing around his chest with joy.

'That was brilliant!' said Rita, as the make-up team rushed in to refresh everybody's faces before the next scene: Bogey doing the 'Shake Your Bogey' dance in front of one of the Eiffel Tower's famous yellow lifts, with Frank, Tiffany, Mum and Dad all bursting out to join in.

'Here, put this on,' said Mike, popping a glittery hat on to Bogey's head as they moved towards the lifts.

But suddenly a crowd of superfans stormed the set:

'Ooh, I can't wait for your TV show,' cried Mrs Wirrel as she shook Frank's and Tiffany's hands. Then she turned to Bogey with a coy look. 'And you? Well, I just love you – eh-hem, I mean . . . I can't wait to see what you'll do in Paris! Shame my poodles can't be here to see it.'

'You don't love him as much as me,' said Walter Wills the grocer, pushing past Mrs Wirrel. 'Will you sign this toma— erm, piece of cheese for me?' He handed Bogey a pen marked *'Plus Grand Fan'* (which means 'number one fan' in French).

Bogey obliged.

'And are you going to star in Mr Pickerty-Boop's new film, *Return of the Sloppy Seine Monster*?' Bo Jacobs the street performer asked Bogey excitedly, as Squishy his dancing hamster tried to attract Bogey's attention by doing ballet on one of the tower's girders.

'And will you say, "goo-goo-gooey" for me?' swooned Mrs Sniff, the Pickerty-Boops' elderly neighbour, waving a postcard she'd just bought.

'**Goo-goo-gooey**,' said Bogey, pretending to jump out at her.

Mrs Sniff giggled so hard she had to sit down.

That's right, stinkers. Once the truth had come out about Bogey, Honkerty's villagers had become HIS BIGGEST FANS and had followed the Snozzlers to all their show spots around the world.

As Frank stood there, watching Bogey chat and laugh with them, in a scene that strangely reminded him of something he'd seen at home not six months before, it warmed his heart.

Whoever would have thought the sight of a snot monster

on the Eiffel Tower could cause such joy?

It was a proper happy ending!

And so, dear stinkers, it's time for us to leave our heroes to their fan club and new TV show. Plus, Fergus the smelly field mouse sent me a whopper box of boiled sprouts last night, so I just need to leave the room for a quick tootle—

Whoops! Sorry! I just did.

Oh well. At least it wasn't because of **THE STINK**.

Can we still be friends?

The End

(for real this time)

EXTRA PICKINGS!

STINK ALERT!
STINK ALERT!

GRAB YOUR NOSE PEGS NOW!

You are about to read Fergus the Smelly Field Mouse's Guide to Whiffy Stuff (which is really another name for Stink- and non-Stink-related farts). I told you not to show this book to grown-ups and now is not the time to start. Most adults hate stinky-squiffs and pouffys and flopdogs (or whatever you want to call a fart), so if they see this guide, they'll take it away.

YOU HAVE BEEN WARNED!

Fergus the Smelly Field Mouse's Guide to Whiffy Stuff

FIZZY-WHIP: *a fast-moving, bubbly fart that pops out in a succession of small explosions. Should you find yourself fizzy-whipping, it is best to move away from any naked flames or your pants might catch fire.*

FLOPDOG: *a slow trump which, as its name suggests, just 'flops' out – rather like a dog 'flopping' on to the floor after a heavy meal. Though unlike real dogs, flopdogs rarely smell, so lucky you!*

FLUFFADORA: *an almost-silent expulsion of air. Don't be fooled – unlike flopdogs, fluffadoras are proper whiffy. In fact, some have been known to knock people out. If you smell one, RUN! Unless it's your own; in which case, grab a nose peg.*

LINK: *a good-natured little bum-pop whose squeaky expulsion makes you and whoever you are with giggle. Its name derives from its ability to create a positive 'link'*

between two or more people.

POUFFY: *an onomatopoeic trumplette that sounds as inoffensive as it is. Pouffys are pleasant little odourless farts that do their owners the world of good by removing unwanted air from their tummies. If you ever have to wish for a fart, wish for a pouffy.*

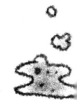

STINKY-SQUIFF: *an embarrassing fart that appears at the worst possible moment – at the doctor's, on crowded buses, in lifts etc. Unfortunately, stinky-squiffs are always so potent that they make your eyes go squiffy – hence the name.*

TE-HE: *a silent fart squeezed out beneath the bedclothes and detectable only when the covers are moved. The name 'te-he' stems from the laughter emitted by the bum-poppers themselves, when others detect the smell and complain.*

TOOTYWINK: *a sneaky little fartlet that's barely a 'pop'. But beware. The initial burst is only the beginning. Once*

the first one's out, it's always followed by more, making your bottom sound like a mini brass band.

WHIFFY-WHIFFY-WOO-WOO: *a misleadingly light trump whose noxious smell lingers in the air for several minutes after its expulsion. As a result, whiffy-whiffy-woo-woos are often used by children to annoy other members of their families.*

WHOOSH-HURDLE: *a very specialist fart used only by dishonest athletes to blow over their opponents' obstacles during hurdle races. If you are whoosh-hurdled by a competitor, it is very hard to prove, as the wind usually carries the fart away, thus destroying the evidence.*

SNOZZLERS OPTION FROM PAGE 26

Gosh, you do like boring stuff! Well you asked for it, so here goes:
After lots of celebrating, the journey back from Warble-Blob was long and tedious and tiring. Once the Snozzlers got back to Honkerty Village at about 11 p.m., they dropped Tiffany off at her house, then everyone went to bed. ZZZ. ZZZ. ZZZ. SNORE. SNORE. SNORE!
BORING!
There. Happy?
Now go back to page 26 and choose the Lobbo option, this time. Honestly!

HOW GOO MAKE BIKKIE-WIKKIES

INGREDIENTS:
- ❋ About 302 g plain flour
- ❋ Roughly 201 g butter
- ❋ Approaching 101 g caster sugar (plus extra for dusting)
- ❋ A few drops of green food colouring

EQUIPMENT NEEDED:
- ❋ Baking tray
- ❋ Large mixing bowl
- ❋ Rolling pin
- ❋ Cookie cutter
- ❋ Greaseproof paper

Line a baking tray with greaseproof paper. Preheat your oven to 170°C/150°C (fan). Plop all the ingredients into a bowl and mix with your fingers 'til you've got a big green, squishy ball (you'll need a grown-up to help, but don't show them this book, remember). Flour a work surface

and your rolling pin, then roll the squishy ball out (gently) until it's 2 cm thick. Use the cookie cutter to make snot blobs - ehem, I mean circles (or whatever shape you've chosen). Sprinkle the snot blobs with a little extra caster sugar. Mark them with 'B'. Then put them in the oven for Bogey and me (sorry, I mean for you) for 20 minutes, or until they just start turning light brown on the edges. Let them cool. Scoff your fear away.

LYRICS

'SHAKE YOUR BOGEY'
Improvised by the Snozzlers

Dance, dance, dance, dance,
dance, dance, dance, dance,
dance!
Shake your bogey!
OW! Shake your bogey!
Dance, dance, dance, dance,
dance, dance, dance, dance,
dance!
Shake your bogey . . .

Goo-goo gooey-goo!
Goo-goo gooey-goo!
Goo-goo gooey-goo!
Goo-goo gooey-goo!

Ah – Shake your bogey!
Ah – Shake your bogey!
Ah – Shake your bogey!
Ah . . . OW!

Dance, dance, dance, dance,
dance, dance, dance, dance,
dance!
Shake your bogey!
OW! Shake your bogey!
Dance, dance, dance, dance,
dance, dance, dance, dance,
dance!
Shake your bogey . . .

Goo-goo gooey-goo!
Goo-goo gooey-goo!
Goo-goo gooey-goo!
Goo-goo gooey-goo!

Ah – Shake your bogey!
Ah – Shake your bogey!
Ah – Shake your bogey!

Shake shake shake shake
shake shake shake shake
. . . OW!

Shake your bogey!
Shake your bogey!

Ah-ah-ah shake your bogey!
Ah-ah-ah shake your bogey!
Oo-oo-oo shake your bogey!
Oo-oo-oo shake your bogey
. . .
AH . . .
AH . . .
AH . . .
AH . . .

Goo-goo gooey-goo!
Shake shake your bogey!
Goo-goo gooey-goo!
Shake shake your bogey!
Goo-goo gooey-goo!
Shake your bogey!
Shake shake shake shake
shake shake shake shake
AH!

ACKNOWLEDGEMENTS

Dear _____

(Insert your name here if it's listed below. This book would not exist without you, so I want to shower you with sno— erm, gratitude.)

And so, a big **THANK GOO** to:

- Sam Copeland, my brilliant agent.
- Rachel Leyshon, my fantabulous editor, who gave Bogey a second book to shake his bogey in.
- Owen Lindsay, the man who brought Bogey to life. I'm in love with your drawings!
- Everybody at Chicken House – Barry Cunningham, Jasmine Bartlett Love, Olivia Jeggo, Rachel Hickman, Esther Waller, Fraser Crichton, Steve Wells – for continuing to believe in my wacky world.
- Ollie Paquin, the best twelve-year-old book promoter an author could wish for.
- My writing family: Annaliese Avery, Yvonne Banham, Sharon Boyle, Sarah Broadley, Adam Connors, Clare Harlow, Urara Hiroeh, Michael Mann, Helen MacKenzie, Angela Murray, Chrissie Sains, Harriet Worrell. You all rock!
- Dan Watts, my ultra-talented co-composer of 'Shake Your Bogey'!
- Xavier Bussy, my friend, musician and (this time around) lender of music recording studio space.
- Gail and Bill, my wonderful parents.
- Pascal and Max, my inspiration. Your love, support and untiring positivity are snot to be sniffed at!

Gooliemaloolie! Thank you everybody!